I Did
You Can Too

One Woman's Motorcycling Adventure

Dorothy Seabourne

 www.trafford.com

North America & international
toll-free: 1 888 232 4444 (USA & Canada)
phone: 250 383 6864 ♦ fax: 812 355 4082

Table of Contents

This book is dedicated to those who said:
"I could",
one who said "Let's do it",
another asked, "Why not?"
and then someone suggested , "Let's meet."
Life would have been less than perfect without those friends.

Life is short, live it and ride it.

Thank you, Ilse. It was you who gave me the key.

This book is also dedicated to my Grandchildren who someday might pick up a copy of this book and know that their Gramma had a life, way back when.

Introduction

Introduction to my World

I was always told that I had a story to tell. I had over 24 years of riding experience. I began to look forward to finding a way to tell my stories in an interesting and an enjoyable way to a reader. The first step was to write the happenings as I remembered and document them. I am an amateur photographer and have taken shots of people, places and anything that would draw my attention. Now I had to put them all together.

Over a number of years I continued with the traveling and photography and in the year 2000 the idea of writing became a reality. To do this type of traveling in America, I mostly rode a Honda Gold Wing. These bikes provided me with comfort, storage, and low maintenance, all necessary qualities for long rides on very long roads.

In North America, the Gold Wings I have owned were a 1976 1000, '82 1100 Interstate, '86 1200 Interstate, '93 1500 Aspencade, and a '99 1500 Aspencade SE, the very best bike yet. I also had a 1994 Honda ST 1100 (oops!) you'll read about that later...

In Europe, I rented a Kawasaki 550, Honda 600 Hurricane, Honda 440 and various sized BMWs. For a few years I owned a BMW K100RT that I kept in the UK.

North American riding was always interesting but European travel took on a whole new meaning to beauty and riding. My favourite area has always been the Swiss Alps. The switchbacks, hairpin curves, the long sweeps all stretched my limits to lay the bike just a wee bit lower in curves and then straighten up to climb even higher. On those roads a feeling of control and capability was always there. Brown Swiss cows grazing on the hills just above me on a curve or tunnels appearing everywhere made me wonder what was around the next bend and the next and the next...

The cost played a big part when renting. I found the smaller bikes more preferable then the North American touring bikes especially in the mountains and the busier highways of Europe. The bigger the bike was the cost of the rental would be more. I wasn't overseas to buy a bike. I just wanted to ride one for a week or two.

My book of memories was an enjoyable challenge. In writing and searching out the right photos, my memories flooded back to the good times and some very sad times. Through it all, I believe I have put together a picture of one person's experiences while on the road.

No full names have been mentioned. The ladies I traveled with will recognize themselves on some trips. My companions were women from all walks of life including a computer analyst, bank manager, Doctor, real estate agent, homemakers, anesthesiologist, tour director and a Nun. Myself, I'm an upholsterer.

My desire for this book is to document the feelings, places, the sad times and the very good times thoroughly. My hope is that you the reader can imagine you are operating the bike as it flew through the mountain passes or rode on the North American highways.

When all is said and done, I can say I was where I wanted to be and wouldn't change one second of those years, except perhaps to turn back the hands of time and start all over again.

So much appreciation goes out to those who encouraged me, gave me praise, critiqued me and refreshed my memories. To Frank, I thank you for your love, encouragement and support during all those years. To Joan, who helped me put my idea together and mainly, for just listening and Ty, for her computer expertise and calm voice. To Audrey for her years as a mentor, a riding companion and good friend, and especially to my dear friend Ilse, without her return phone call to a 'newbie', this book would not have reached page one.

Reasons to travel

Photographers dream of the sunrises we see around our pond in the early mornings. The sun reflects its sleepy face in the water as the gray heron's shadow illuminates an eerie show of still shapes. A doe and her fawn travel a well-worn path along the outskirts of our property. With all the wonder that surrounds me, why would I travel? The reason is simple. With this much beauty in my back yard, what else could there be?

My husband is a hobby farmer who also works 40 hours outside of the home. His love of the land can be traced back to his childhood, living on a working family farm in Essex County, Southern Ontario. A day in the field brings him more satisfaction then any well paid job. He knows where the areas' coyotes might be playing or the nighttime bedding of deer. He also brings me cloves of wild garlic or bouquets of wild flowers and has said, 'weeds are just flowers growing in the wrong place.' With all that I have at home my reasons are simple, I've always been curious. I want to see different customs, taste exotic foods and buy unusual clothes. I photograph the areas I have traveled through and with my memories show him what else is out there.

His support has been monumental to my well being on the road. There was an occasion when I had to deal with a tragedy on the road and just to hear his voice helped me calm down with the ongoing situation around me. It has been fortunate that my own bikes have given me no trouble on the road and I'm sure he's comfortable with that knowledge...

Many times I've heard of girls having terrible bike problems. They would be left in a motel waiting for parts to be delivered. My disadvantage, I don't know how to repair a bike and I'm left to the mercy of dealerships and mechanics. I've been heard often to say 'I ride them, I don't fix them.' With proper maintenance, my Wings have given me this choice.

My longest trips have been 3 to 4 weeks and as much as I enjoy traveling, after the third week I get antsy to be home, back to what I call normal. So why do I travel? I've thought that if I had to explain, there would be no point. They could never understand....

Short time not a long time

My, my. You've come a long way lady!

I remember when I couldn't drive and then, learning to drive anything was a challenge. The first car I drove was a '56' Pontiac. To get your license in those days was relatively simple compared to the more stringent standards of today, which I applaude whole-heartedly. In those days of course, there was not as much traffic. All I remember was driving around a block or two, parallel parking one time, backing the car up to a gate, then driving a few blocks back to the license bureau. I then had a license.

In the early 80's, I had a wide variety of vehicles to drive, and yet sitting in our garage was the one thing I had yet to take out on the road – alone.

She was a 1976 yellow Honda Gold Wing left behind for our use by Frank's younger brother. He was moving to Alberta riding a '79' Honda CBX and said he couldn't ride two at a time so we could ride her or park her.

Frank and I doubled up on weekends and rode with friends but I was never satisfied as a 'pillion' so I decided to take the big step and go after my motorcycle license.

At a family wedding I met the mother of the best man who said she wanted to get her license too. We agreed to sign up for the safety course together. I arrived on the due date to find she had backed out. I was a woman alone on my quest with a number of new male riders.

We had a choice of bikes to ride and I chose the Honda 200. It was a tall bike and with my height, I thought it could be an advantage for me. For a new rider-to-be with no riding history whatsoever, the lessons were challenging but I stubbornly persevered. The fact that I had ruined a brand new pair of boots, (*kick starting did them in*) to not get my license at that point would be unacceptable.

Those few days seemed so long. It didn't help that one was a very, very rainy session but we repeated exercises over and over again until we got it right. My favourite was the teeter-totter, but learning hand signals was not and I was retested for that specific reason. I didn't have a bike to practice on except 'Ole Yaller' and at the time her size was overpowering to me.

After 20 hours of riding lessons along with a lot of blood, sweat and tears, I earned my license and it opened a brand new world to me – the world of Motorcycle Riding.

Now I felt 2 feet taller (*in my mind*), so capable, a-n-d nervous, but once on the road - Oh the freedom!

I was 43 years old. I could ride a motorcycle and I was no longer a passenger!

My first bike to ride was the Wing. With a lot of practice on side streets and industrial malls in the months to follow, I learned to handle this wonderful beast. My goal at the time was to ride down Clifton Hill, the busiest touristy street in Niagara Falls. I knew that if I could do that, I was ready for the highways.

Now with my license, my next objective was to find someone other than my husband to ride with. I actively searched for other lady riders.

I started by attending motorcycle races. I even advertised on the radio for any lady who might be interested in riding with a new rider. I received one call.

Ilse was a sweet Austrian Lady who lived ½ hour away from me and she agreed to meet me to biker talk. We met (*at a dairy bar – what else?*) and over the following years we traveled together to many local activities and rides. Along with the many lessons learned on the road, she taught me how to get on my bike like a lady. I never knew there was a different way. It was also because of this special lady that I met the Motor Maids.

During those years the Bob Harpwood Memorial Anniversary rides were being held at the Welland County Motorcycle Club. The Motor Maids were invited to celebrate the occasion by parading around the track. My soon to be lifelong friend, Audrey extended an invitation for the ladies to stay at her home during that weekend.

I couldn't believe the distances these ladies traveled and the bikes! Every bike ever put on the road was there. One year Audrey had 52 girls register so her backyard looked like tent city. I was so impressed and joined the club then or soon after. Many of the ladies I met that year are still close friends. I found the Motor Maids were to be an extension of a family I chose to join.

It took twenty-some years to get to this stage and here I am at the best time of my life.

I now ride a 99 White Gold Wing and marvel that Honda can keep making them better. I feel I have the best bike on the road - *for me anyways.*

I don't know if I could pinpoint the best of these riding years. I have so many good memories but with the best came some of the saddest, with the loss of riding companions through accidents and time.

I have an empty spot deep in the core of my heart when I remember the friends I have lost. Some are no longer on the earthly trips I relish every day, but I believe they are the Angels who travel with me and have shown their presence many times.

Each ride I take, I give thanks to my 'God' for their presence and one more day, plus having the ability to ride, in these very special times.

When riding the passes of Austria I remember Nancy/Florida and myself, flying down mountains that included the Alps, Pyrenees and the Dolomites.

I think of Joan/Ontario and myself chasing the sun down outside of Chico California, stopping, putting on a jacket and then retracing our short wild ride back to the Hotel.

I have memories of Arlene/Ohio and myself following each other in synch, winding the curvy roads in Northern Ontario that were meant for our travels.

Audrey/Ontario always in the lead, riding her Harley like a pro and teaching me most of what I know today. Audrey was a good teacher and she is my friend.

All these memories are forever engraved in my mind and knowing I was the lucky one who could call them 'friend.' What more could I ask for?

We were put on this earth for a good time, not a long time. Lucky is the person who can say they lived it and they weren't alone.

Learning the Ropes

37 F – 6:45am

As the early morning sun cut through the mist over the pond, she looked even more spectacular. Her colour was of the purest white pearl with her chrome shining like a multitude of mirrors AND she was running! The dewdrops on her paint glistened with the exhaust blowing its own mystical haze around her. She was ready!

Our Motor Maid Breakfast was only two hours away. Having mentioned to another friend that I wasn't sure if I would be making the trip, her magic words were "it all depends on just how bad we wanted to go." We always did like a challenge.

Her name was 'Ghost' a '99' white Gold Wing with most everything known to man to allow a touring bike to be the best. She had heated grips, a hookup for electric gloves, gel seat, C.B., temp gauge, reverse, and most important to me, a stereo system that would rival any home stereo in existence.

The name 'Ghost' was a euphemism for my reputation of taking off, away from any situation that was unacceptable to me. Purchased in October, there weren't too many rides left for a Canadian Bike(r) in this season, so we were antsy. This was her debut to fellow riders.

Magic times! Warm hands - warm body - full gas tank - and wonderful music and it's only 37 F – 6:45 in the morning…

Different Stages of Maturity

At the age of 43, I began another direction in my life that would last over 25 years and still counting. I might have settled down with satisfaction in my comfortable life but I was still curious about the new-to-me possibilities while riding a motorcycle. Many thought and asked if I was trying to get my youth back. It was never about getting it back. I wanted to enhance all the good things and riding gave me that opportunity.

My children were almost grown up. I had more time to devote to my husband, myself and this new sport. I still had to work and maintain a household but the weekends were times to ride, find more female riders and places to go.

The first Club I joined was the Motor Maids and if I had a good time 'it was all, their fault', and I say, "thank you so very much." Weekends then included trips to New York State, Michigan and occasionally Ohio along with side trips all over Ontario.

The many miles brought backaches (solved with a back rest) and headaches (induced by anxiety as a new rider). Weather also played a big part until I learned which clothes worked in the rain and cold, and what did not. Time took care of a lot of things.

Items that were 'tried and found true' included man-made padded jackets and pants that were all weather items. Leather will always look great but when cold and wet, looks did nothing for my well being. Lucky for me the colour attracted me to this line of clothing and it was to be most functional in wet and cold weather. With that came electric gloves, since electric grips only warmed my palms, my fingertips were cold most of the time. Now with proper clothing I could extend my Canadian season by a number of precious weeks… Waterproof boots and a flip up full face helmet completed my riding gear for all weather. I could put complete focus on the road and deal comfortably with less-than-perfect weather. All these items were not purchased overnight and I had to experience the bad to know the good. When I hit the road, I know that except for ice and snow, there are very few days I can't ride. It just depends on how much I want to go. 37 F and 6:45am can be a great ride.

My first longest trip was to a Motor Maid Convention in Yakima Washington. I was fortunate to have a seasoned rider to follow and learn the rules of the road. She showed me the proper way to handle my front brakes on wet construction roads, and I have never forgotten. You do not touch them on any wet surface, especially going downhill.

21 years since that trip, I have accumulated 223,000 miles and am still counting.

I survived and learned during those first years. There have been so many roads, sometimes I think my brain goes into overload because there's just too much to remember. What I do remember; makes me want to go back and there are places I have visited more than once. So many places, so little time but the time I have spent was worth it.

A dear friend once said, "If you have your health, you have everything. Money is the easiest to get." At this point in my life I have the health and with good luck there will be many more places to go. My only enemy at this point IS time but you can bet I'll make the most of it.

White Hair and Patience

The rumble of bike engines, a flash of chrome and the parking lot becomes the center of attention as the riders dismount their wings of steel. Beneath their helmets emerges, hair colours varying from the dark grays to shades of white. They are lady riders!

In the not-so-distant past it was expected that riders might certainly be male but not anymore. Now with the resurgence of motorcycles in the past years, the number of lady riders is rising at a phenomenal rate. No longer content to ride as a passenger, women are now more commonly the operator of these magnificent machines. To see women on the largest of bikes on the road has become a common sight. Eventually if she wants to travel extensively she may find it necessary to have a ride that fits her touring needs. With that come the needs of more storage and a more powerful motorcycle for a more comfortable long distance ride. Any bike can achieve this, although even a touring bike with all the goodies, after many miles can be uncomfortable. Bigger doesn't always find resolution to all problems.

With the number of women's clubs available now, there is a wealth of information accessible to the new rider. That info provides links to other women who are also seeking companionship and support for this new-found hobby. There are advantages to having a companion that is a like-minded person. First they are not alone on the road, sharing the cost of lodging is more reasonable and above all it's more fun with someone.

The number of white haired ladies having ridden for many years is becoming more common. The attention given to these riders can sometimes be more than funny. I've seen many times people will just

6

stop to watch us maneuver the bikes in a parking lot and then of course some have questions. Questions like; how long have we been riding? How heavy is the bike? (*I didn't plan on carrying it*) How far did we travel and if they didn't see *us* park the bikes, ask us if our husbands are with us to drive the bike. Fortunately (for them), we haven't been asked how old we are too many times but I was told once, 'it's not expected to see women of your age operating a motorcycle.'(Germany) I wonder what is normal now.

There is admiration and with the silly questions I've had some interesting conversations with couples, especially the men. I think because we operate our own bike, we can relate to problems and issues most non-riders do not understand. Most of the time, men admire women who ride and if at our age we are still riding then we must really know what we're doing. I want to believe that anyway. I admit that as I get older there are some changes. Being more cautious and aware becomes more acute. The love of the freedom and feeling so capable is like an aphrodisiac. The more you get, the more you want. When the season changes and you can't ride, anticipation becomes more intense. Your mind plays games as to when and how far you can go the next time.

Winters are especially long for Northern riders so the lucky ones might become 'snowbirds' and head south for a break. The goal generally is to get there but if you're lucky you can take your bike too, others are not so lucky. For the rest of us non-snowbirds we know the weather will change but we must be patient. In the meantime, we have Bike Shows to attend. Club meetings and breakfasts are good reasons to bike-talk.

Myself, I'll have to be one of the patient ones. I've been told, all I need is one good day to ride south and I'll be in the warmer temps. Now that might just be an option. Hmmm…

The days - they are getting shorter

Looking outside I know there's not a lot of daylight left. I have to do something else besides work. Is that sunshine beneath those grey clouds? Yes! It is! There is some time to enjoy this fading, fall day. Frank suggests I get out while the *gitten* is good so... Wouldn't it be great if someone else thinks the same thing? That person could be looking at the same clouds, tired of the mundane duties and if prompted, she might want to meet somewhere? Yes I do know a rider who has mentioned numerous times the freedom she felt on the road, just riding. There isn't a road too long or too short, if the opportunity is there.

I should dress for cooler weather (my favourite time of year). I'll put on my all -weather riding jacket and pants and mid size gloves. With the electric grips I'll be prepared and warm for this impromptu ride.

One short phone call later she agrees to meet at Tim Horton Donuts in Dunnville, Ontario. *Where did we go before Timmies?*

The 'Ghost' is warming up. I'm plugged in. Josh Grobin is singing "You lift me up," (so apropos) and riding out my tree-lined driveway, I'm on the road and I'm free!

The oncoming fall presents tree branches losing their last sign of foliage and paints the land with a multitude of red, gold's and orange colours. Leaves are blown aside as I whiz through them and boast of a beautiful time of year that is fleeing with my every breath.

Field corn stands limp, waiting for the farmer or winter to take it down - whichever happens first. In the pastures, horses stand with their winter fur, backs to the wind providing insulation against the oncoming cold. Pumpkins abound everywhere. Every size pumpkin available is seen in road-side stalls ready for Halloween decorations in the next few days. Some are just left in the fields -waiting.

Dunnville is a busy little town, growing by leaps and bounds. It is approx. 45 minutes away from home and probably the same time/distance for my friend. Meeting at Timmy's we get some curious looks but we also know that for many, we are doing what they wish they could. We know we're fortunate and wouldn't be anywhere else in the world in this space in time.

Watching my friend walk across the parking lot with all her warm riding gear, it's difficult to see (her mouth is covered by a neck/scarf) if she is smiling underneath all that gear or... Whew! She's smiling!!!

We talk about the up and coming Convention in 2006. The possibility of rides in the next year and then just enjoy our coffee while looking out the window, watching the *rain* fall. Well there were no guarantees it wouldn't rain. I've heard from "God's mouth to some one's ears" we're not made of sugar and won't melt. Not comforting words when it's cooling off and getting wetter by the minute but luck held and the rain did stop.

A half hour or so later, gearing up, (this time with electric gloves) we wipe the rain off our seats, say our goodbyes and head back home. Who would have thought years ago that so many grand and great-grandmothers would be traveling on their own motorcycles? My how times have changed!

As we were leaving the parking lot, a female O.P.P. (Police) officer gives us thumbs up, reassuring us that we weren't the only ones' who knew we were lucky.

As usual, I wander home on different roads. One might wonder with so much beauty around us, why travel so far, so often? I have thought that if there is this much to see and experience this close, what else is out there? We all need that shot of adrenalin to keep us alert, knowing that our long non-riding winter season is peaking around the corner.

It is an absolute joy to ride solo but to have a like-minded companion, the bonus is to meet each other after stealing those few sweet hours, and ride.

That's what it's all about, the freedom, the friendship and the RIDE.

Why wouldn't anyone be envious?

Under the Canal

The sun was warm as the fall leaves blew across our paths and our five bikes cut through, sending them flying up and over us. This would probably be one of the last rides of our northern fall season and so far it was perfect.

After I had made a number of calls to a few Canadian girls, we arranged to meet another girl from Rochester in a hamlet named Barker, NY, along the southwestern shore of Lake Ontario. We knew this would not be a marathon ride but we had to get out and go somewhere. Barker was chosen as our meeting point.

The ride was 1½ hours time-wise and the food at our chosen restaurant was good. After some conversation we had to start heading home. Of course we would be creative in our trip home and our American friend suggested we might go *under* a canal for a change - the Erie Barge Canal. I had been over it and around it but not under. It was an especially short tunnel but we did take some pictures and then parted company.

Our friend headed east to Rochester, NY while we continued west, back toward the bridges to Canada. In that area there are four. The sun was still brilliant as leaves of red and yellow maples painted the landscape leading us to Goat Island and the Three Sisters Islands. There the rivulets of fast running water surged into the main waters falling off the brink of Niagara Falls. The scene was spectacular standing beside those treacherous waters. It was interesting to me that in all the years I had lived in the Niagara Falls area, I had never been this close to the American Falls. Words don't describe how

11

overpowering the water felt standing so close. One girl did say it was awesome and that word just might fit.

Three or four of our group climbed down to the rocks along the water's edge while some took photos. After a few minutes we were off once again headed for the Rainbow Bridge at Niagara Falls.

As we tip-toed through to customs we generally attract attention from people sitting in cars admiring the bikes. There are a few thumbs–up, some chatter and maybe second looks from those not realizing until they get close, we were all women!

Most people like their creature comforts when the weather is less than perfect and then others stand in awe at the difference. Right then the weather was perfect for motorcycles and I'm sure there are those who would want to trade places with us. Given different circumstances they would be just as content to stay in their 4 wheeled cages. There are times we wish that too. Right then, there was not enough money to want to trade.

This moment we longed for happened because of that final 'kick at the can' before the long winter months settle in. One more memory, we can thank each rider for a great day.

Anyone care to 'kick that can again?' Call a friend and watch what happens.,.

Spring time (up close and personal)

The fear-driven dilated eye, a spotty coarse and smooth coat but especially the sound of the hooves softly thudding on the pavement across my path, I remember. This close encounter of a young buck was but a split second, yet long enough for me to never forget the eye. As quickly as the incident happened, the animal was gone and the only words out of my mouth were "Thank you God!" "That was close enough!"

Spring is a wonderful time of year for all species. It is a time of new beginnings, growth, reproducing and for a few of us, the NEED to be on the road again. Nature is at her best at this time of year. It's the time cows are giving birth, ducks laying eggs but also the time deer are moving and you might just cross paths...

It's also a dangerous time. This time too, more bikes are on the same secondary roads and a rider must be in tune to his/her surroundings because when you are on the move, so are they.

A group of our Ladies' first outing of the season that year took us on a ride through farm country in Southern Ontario. Ever aware of the few buffalo grazing in the pasture, a large dog suddenly jumped out of the ditch beside us and darted in front of my front wheel. The dog was so close and fast that I do believe I ran over the tip of its tail. The rider behind me said when the dog passed in front of me it yipped and seemed to accelerate even faster to the opposite side of the road. If my wheel did get him, I wondered later if the scare would keep the dog away from the road. It probably wouldn't.

13

This incident happened so fast. Uppermost in my mind was to not drop the bike and for a short wee second I held on tighter. I tried not to go out of our staggered formation in front or behind another bike and especially not into the ditch. Luckily nothing happened but that was just plain good old-fashioned luck or even one of my Angels at work.

That day the birds even seemed suicidal swooping down on the lead bike at times. It was just a crazy but lucky day for everyone including the dog and myself.

This ride we had ten or so girls of various riding skills. The group occasionally separated, in a way so the 'newbies' could get used to traveling as a group. Perhaps find a friend they would be compatible to ride with. For all my riding years I had been truly fortunate to have had the same person to ride with. I learned many valuable lessons in those years. Others are sometimes not so lucky. It all depends on the rider.

This was our first ride of the season and hopefully there will be many more to come this new year. I just don't want to be quite so "up close and personal" with the critters while on any of our rides. I can only hope.

Mice – curses of curses

It was like a cartoon – only this was the real thing. Mouse Time in the country. There she was, Mom attached to six babies jumping from my bike and then taking off into the field. 28 legs if you can believe that! Watching the antics, my friend (who will remain nameless) just sat on her bike and laughed and laughed as I backed my bike out of the shed. I don't want to repeat the one word I used.

That summer was especially problematic. They were more particular that year. They chose my bike for their home or nest or whatever and why not, the trip trunk?

One time I opened the back trunk to find a new box of Kleenex twice as high and inside a whole family of baby mice. We also found soybeans in the air-breather that my husband had to seal off with light screening and bits of foam in Mom's nest so the War Is On.

With the mice using my bike as their home they also used it as a toilet. When my bike was warming up, the smell of dirty hygiene was totally unacceptable.

I normally park my Wing in a specially built shed big enough to park two bikes but now there is only one. The other side of the shed was full of miscellaneous articles stored for various seasons and for some reason the bike was more acceptable to raise a family *(of mice -what else?)*

I bought everything known to man to get rid of them. I bought poison but they must have taken it with them because there was never any left.

If we did get rid of any of the pesky critters there was always a cousin and its family around somewhere. At some point something bigger than a mouse must have gotten an awful sore tummy because it took the whole cube. We tried mothballs but all that did was make everything smell like mothballs. What else is new? It seemed the only thing left was sticky -traps. They can work if the mice step in them but if you saw them there, would you? I don't think so and neither did they.

A poor frog did and I promptly set it loose along with a variety of bugs but no mice.

Sticky traps in themselves I suppose are good for something but they were never meant to be anywhere around my Wing or any bike for that matter. Backing the bike out, I thought I could go straight back and the wheel would go past the trap. Instead it went over the edge and now it was stuck to the side of my tire. I got off the bike, removed the trap and continued to back out and headed down the driveway. The sound of my (normally quiet) Wing going down a gravel driveway with all the clattering loose stones flying off my wheel is to say the least, aggravating and NOT funny.

Eventually I discovered a gizmo at Canadian Tire called an Electrical Mouse Deterrent. Plugged in, it gives off a light or sound that frightens mice, so far, so good.

This year has been relatively free of mice. In talking to a mechanic, the worst case scenario is that they will chew into wires. Down the road there might be serious problems you really didn't need…Sooooo… (like I said) the war is on.

There is nothing more aggravating then to see a family vacate my bike…when they weren't even invited in the first place.

16

Embarrassing Moments

As a newer rider and riding one of the larger touring bikes, there were lessons to learn along with aggravating experiences meant to happen. In 1988, our MM Convention was held in Peterborough Ontario and as soon as it was over my traveling companions and I headed for the Maritime Provinces.

One Sunday at a local breakfast many years later the conversation reminded me of an incident that still makes me smile. That trip was a real adventure. I was going to travel to the most eastern side of North America and experience the difference of our cultures with the kindness of our Eastern Province riders. The trip was not without difficulty though.

Soon into the trip an electrical problem plagued my companion's bike. This was the second time for it to quit only this time in Cornerbrook Newfoundland. At that point she'd already had an expensive visit to a garage in New Brunswick to replace an electrical wiring harness. Our Nova Scotia friends might have a better solution.

My friend could take her bike to the Halifax/Dartmouth area. Her bike was a Harley FXRST and the Hell's Angels in Halifax were well known for their expertise in repairing Harleys. After a long ferry ride from Newfoundland to North Sydney Nova Scotia, (*not her favourite way to travel*) riders loaded her bike into a van and took it to Halifax. A couple hours of waiting in the bike shop, she then had to ride back late that same night to Sydney NS.

She arrived home hours later making that one of the longest days on our trip. She left her riding clothes on, crawled into bed and didn't

17

move for the next 24 hours. My friend said she'd never been so tired. A few days later we were on the road again, and her bike performed at 100% for the rest of the trip. The Hell's Angels mechanics DID know what to do.

While taking a solo ride that same day, another companion dropped her Wing on sand close to a Marina. Badly bruising the arch of her foot she had to seek medical assistance from the local hospital.

Gravel, tight curves but mostly hills, and myself a less than experienced rider, I had to learn the hard way. Many years later I know now, when a bike starts to go down, you let it go. *That's assuming you have a choice.* Wrenching your back only hurts you. Your bike can be fixed. Lack of concentration and inexperience could be the culprit.

That Sunday morning at our breakfast years later, Chedicamp Nova Scotia was mentioned and the one thing I remembered was that everything was built on a hill. The Motel was at the top of the *hill*, the office was on the front of the *hill* and turning around on that same *hill* became a test! After a long days ride and trying to turn my "86" Wing around in that parking lot 'we' lost our balance and over we went. The noise of the throttle revving at a high pitch as she went down was a telling sound to my companions. My Wing was in trouble. Just as suddenly all motion stopped and together, my companions and I managed to get her up.

My bike was almost upside down but no damage was done and I'll never forget the image of her from the bottom end up. The whole crazy scene reminded me of a red grasshopper with chrome legs.

Funny now… but not then…

Black was a Beauty...ST 1100

A photographer/rider will always be looking for that perfect picture of her ride. Black Beauty was her name. A 1994 Honda ST 1100, an absolute beauty for the short time I owned her. On that day, our pond looked like the perfect back drop for that 'perfect' shot.

I carefully positioned her near the pond and the lighting was good. I backed away from her. As soon as I had taken a few steps backwards, I could hear the unmistakable sound of grass roots breaking. The 'Beauty' in slow motion, gently started to lean and lean and lean... I had forgotten to put a plate beneath the side stand.

These touring bikes weigh almost half a ton, too heavy for me to pick up. Disgusted with myself, I left her and went back to work. The internal war going on in my head, told me I couldn't pick her up and if she lay there all day, so be it. No one was going to get hurt and she certainly wasn't bothering anyone but me - so there!

Later that day a 6 foot plus delivery person was making a delivery. I sheepishly asked him if he would mind helping me pickup her up. He did say that he thought the bike looked different out there. I thought "of course it was different. Bikes are usually standing up, not lying down!!!"

When a bike goes down for any reason, at first there is concern for damage, then feeling stupid but mostly it's the embarrassment. You forget that it will/can happen, but how is the question. When the bike is standing still then falls the results may not be damaging but when the bike is moving that is another story. In this case the 'Beauty' was

19

stopped and all this nonsense for the sake of a picture. Some reasons, really can't justify the end results.

One short note is of a Michigan Motor Maid of slight stature dropping her motorcycle at a set of lights. As small as she was and angry, she managed to pick up her bike and almost threw it over into the ditch. Now that was adrenalin and temper pumping at a high pitch.

There are so many stories out there ready for the telling. I certainly have mine.

Heading South

Ignorance can be bliss 2005

The 'Ghost' had mixed emotions that year as she traveled to the East Coast Maritimes and it was mainly due to the ignorance of a few and the kindness of others.

Ghost has experienced many elements of life on the road, and she has also learned a thing or two about those who drive on it.

When riding with her CB turned on, she occasionally monitors the truckers for road info and sometimes entertainment. Some of the drivers do have a different way of communicating to others. Most of them talk normal but then there are some with mouths on them you would wonder, how do they eat with them? Some of the 'normal' drivers consider the mouthy ones, a joke and quite often don't turn their CB's on for that reason. It can be embarrassing for them too.

The majority of these drivers are hard working people and like most of us, they have to make a living. The Highways of America can be a test for all just keeping up with speeds, driving long hours and dealing with the weather. For the truckers, they do all of this while handling the largest vehicle on the road. With that being said, who and what is driving amongst us all, is the unknown.

Knowing this, the 'Ghost' could imagine the last thing these truckers might want would be bikers traveling too close to them. Cutting in and out or just being a little slower than some of the semis. Most of the time good drivers of all vehicles know what is expected of them.

21

During the many miles the 'Ghost' has ridden, she has been witness to a lot of stupidity from both types of drivers. The many acts of kindness shown over-shadowed the negativity.

When riding through the Maritimes that year, she and her companions were positively helped, in many different ways. When traffic gave them reason to question what might be going on in front of them the CB was access to info from other drivers. They would pass on info concerning construction, stalled traffic or even why traffic was being diverted in another direction. Most of the time, the response was positive and helpful.

Help can also come in different forms especially in bad storms and fog. At the worst of times it has been known that truckers have traveled close to bikers, beside them or ahead of them, protecting them with their size.

A lady friend from Ohio spoke of being shielded from horrendous winds late one evening while traveling along a desolate stretch of the Pacific Trans-Coastal Highway. The driver positioned his transport beside her for a long stretch, preventing the wind from blowing her off the road. "If not for him", she has said," She knows, she would have gone over the edge into the blackness of that night."

Negativity for the 'Ghost' one hot steamy day on the Trans Canada Highway, was hearing a yappy trucker mention 'taking out' three riders who were merging on to the same Causeway in New Brunswick. The 'Ghost' was one of the three.

There wasn't much that could be done to prevent anything from possibly happening, but she did say over her CB, "Please don't," For a few sweet moments she no longer heard his voice. She'd like to think that he had a conscience when he heard *her* voice.

Another incident on that trip, she once again heard the threat of splattering some riders on the highway that day. Hearing the truck drivers comment 'Ghost' quickly moved as far away from a convoy of five same-named transports.

It can be scary on those roads and maybe hearing such talk was not meant to be, but it happened and it's in those moments she wished she did not have a CB. All that being said, the number of good deeds far outweighed the number of irresponsible words and the acts of a few. It's the good we'd like to remember.

It can be dangerous out there and on occasion, not knowing can be bliss.

Yakima Washington

Sometimes it only takes a word, a phrase or a moment to highlight an otherwise testy day. Yakima Washington was the 1986 site for the Motor Maids Annual Convention and my longest ride to date. My companion, a seasoned rider of many years, and I but a novice, were to travel together. I had so much to learn.

Another new Motor Maid had only 100 miles on her motorcycle license that year and was riding a Honda 250 when she headed west from Toronto. I wasn't the only newbie on the block, a BIG block.

I'm still awestruck when I remember how massive Canada is. It would take 2 days to get out of Ontario alone, 1 or 2 days to ride through the prairies and as the land changed it ascended into the Rocky Mountains and British Columbia.

With the number of miles we would be traveling, we would of course experience a variety of weather changes. Especially as we rode into the Mountain range that included passes, long ominous tunnels and windy roads along the Fraser Canyon.

It wasn't uncommon to see bicycle riders, wrapped in green garbage bags in an effort to stay dry. We couldn't imagine riding the bicycles although those riders were probably warmer than we were with their adrenalin moving faster than ours as they peddled up the mountain.

One day I remember so clearly, we were riding into Lake Louise during a rainstorm up a wet dirt construction road. I was so scared! Riding up the road was fine but the thoughts of coming back down put knots in my stomach. A few words of wisdom from my friend, 'don't touch your front brakes coming down', and it worked.

We found out later we could have taken an alternate route but it was information, too little, too late.

My worst enemy throughout my riding career has always been the front brakes. I would learn though as the years went by. We all do but for some, it's the hard way.

Days on that trip seemed so long. We had to travel x number of miles to reach the Convention on booked days. Some days were 3 to 4 hundred mile days and a number of others added up in the 5 to 6 hundred mile range.

As comfortable as my Gold Wing was, after those longer days, parts of my body complained. There were days I would climb off my bike, lay on the ground and stretch or just walk around thinking that child birth didn't hurt this much. Like everything else, eventually the pain went away with a backrest and a softer seat eliminating most of it.

Ladies riding then was sometimes an oddity. Yes, there are some men who will never get used to lady riders on the road, especially, without a man who could help us, ride with us or protect us! Imagine that! Nice that some still think of us as the fragile ones. Interesting too, the conclusions some people make. One day, not paying attention to one car traveling our route, we all pulled into the same restaurant. After a little chit -chat, the couple referred to our being on bikes and especially the fact we were women! His reasoning for our being alone on the road was that he KNEW we were professionals. He knew that, because we traveled so well together. "YUP, that's us, the professionals" ha ha, I didn't know I could follow that good.

25

Another day on that trip after an awful cold wet morning we finally stopped at a McDonald's near Vancouver. We changed into dry clothes, cleaned ourselves up and had our lunch. While we were getting ready to leave, a man came out and was surprised to see that (his words), "those big beautiful bikes were being ridden by women!" Imagine that!!! He said he expected to see two burly sized men and we were 'women!' He looked at my companion and said "My God, you could be my Mother!"

As we walked away out of earshot she commented, "He didn't look like a spring chicken himself."

So many "moans and groans" about the weather, careless drivers and distance. Isn't it interesting that the parts that colour our every trip are the few words spoken?

Boot Hill and who's stubborn?

Bars and restaurants located along the main drag in Daytona were just beginning to open. Delivery trucks and empty parking lots told us that this was not the time to expect too many establishments would be open but the Boot Hill Saloon was. Traffic at this time of the day was sparse compared to the activity in a few hours. The streets would then come alive with motorcycle riders parading this world renowned road, creating a moving mass of leather, helmeted riders of all ages and mannerism. This was Bike Week in Daytona 1999.

At this moment though, I was one of three ladies being refused entry to a worn out bar in this famous city. The thirty-some young man standing at the door was of average build, wearing the typical black t-shirt with Daytona 1999 on the front along with the Saloon's logo. The time was still early so he was freshly shaven and wore a bandana with a tattoo of barbed wire around his upper arm.

At first we didn't think our vests might offend someone but we soon found out that was not the case. Who our vests represented probably didn't matter to him either. He did have rules to enforce so whether we were the Red Devils or the Motor Maids, we couldn't wear our 'colours' inside.

As we entered the bar he matter-of-factly said," Sorry Ma'am, no colours can come in." Stepping back and amused I said "You are kidding, right?", "No Ma'am, it's the rules." "But I could be your Mother or even your Grandmother!" I answered astonished that someone would question our motives. He said, "They couldn't wear their colours either, Ma'am."

27

In defense of the young man, he was polite and dealing with us could have been testy or funny depending on how *he* handled the situation but we felt no offense and it was his job......

For some, being a biker is a way of life and for those not in the 'life' perhaps it's hard to understand what it's all about. Any hobby will bring out the best and worst of people and some of the worst in the biker world are sometimes referred to as the 1%ers. Daytona is all about motorcycling. The racers, the riders, the clothing, the new bikes and the not so new and then there are the 1%ers.

They are the riders who cause trouble for others with fights, the three 'D's (drags, drinking and drugs), and clashes amongst the clubs. It's because of the clashes amongst Renegade clubs, that the bars have the right to refuse entrance to anyone wearing a colour.

For the uninformed, a vest colour signifies who and what club you belong too. Our vests are white with a logo of the Motor Maids emblazoned on the back along with each girl's city and state/province on it. Quite harmless considering ours is the oldest women's club in America and has the reputation of being one of the best.

So now here I stood being refused entrance to this old warn out bar in Daytona. I asked him "Would you be upset if I said that to take my vest off wasn't worth the drink?" He said "No Ma'am, just following the rules, Ma'am." I can say we weren't too offended and we walked away laughing about the notoriety we would have once our members found out. Of course we would tell *someone. Some people just don't get it, we had our rules too.*

Daytona Reality Check

To those who love Motorcycling, the roar or purr of the engines in traffic could be music to the ears. When something goes wrong and the sounds are of metal colliding with metal or the throttle revving up, then for those in the know, a bikers' worst nightmare may have just happened.

When sport bikes are weaving in and out of traffic, it's frightening to everyone and most people pray nothing happens. To be a witness to the consequence of two bikes touching then crashing; is gut wrenching.

This was the first time I actually witnessed an accident and my first thoughts were "Please God, don't let anyone be seriously injured."

Try and picture three young riders wearing shorts, loose sleeveless muscle shirts and sandals instead of boots plus riding super fast bikes. The clothing was all wrong to start with, but to be weaving in and out of heavy traffic during Daytona Bike week was not only the exuberance of youth speaking but plain stupidity. This could be a good reason for some parents to not want their children to ever ride a motorcycle.

The poor judgment of one rider caused his bike to touch another in the group of three bikes as they darted in and out of slow moving cars. The first bike and rider slid down on his side. Off to the side of the road and uninjured, he picked his bike up and rode on at a slower pace. While at almost the same speed the 2nd bike slid off down into the ditch. He too picked himself up and followed the bike to retrieve it. Traffic had stopped at that point.

The bike was pushed out of a shallow ditch, righted and ridden off, following the first rider. The 3rd rider missed being involved in the mishap and continued on unscathed throughout all the action.

I'm sure two riders that night would be nursing some road rash. Relieved that they weren't badly injured I kept thinking that if it would have been one of us, we would feel the pain a lot longer than the young fellows would.

Ah to be young and invincible! We will have at least one reality check in our riding career but for some unfortunately they might not learn...

Americade 2002 – Lake George, NY

The word Americade can be an escape for some. To others it's a well-known rally in Lake George, NY. The rally attracts riders from all over North America and distant countries around the World. The setting is in the Adirondack Mountains in upper New York State. Knowing those great winding roads, the four of us were prompted to attend the rally again.

The 'aphrodisiac' this time was the knowledge that for a few days we could have this precious time together enjoying wonderful roads that just might ease some of the family pressures back home.

One of our girls was having a difficult time with an aging, failing husband. Even though he was given the best of care from the physicians, family and friends, his behaviour was slowly wearing her self-esteem and energy down. At the advice of her physician, it was suggested she take a few days away and perhaps the trip might bring her health back into focus.

That day though, as much as she loved riding there was something different. She was distracted and we could see it. We found out later that morning, unknown to her, a telephone had been installed in her bike. At anytime (when her CB was on) any family member could call her just by dialing her cell phone. Her going on this trip and not having to answer phone calls from anyone was one of the reasons the Doctor suggested she go away. Once she found the connections, she disconnected the phone and no more phone calls could reach her while riding during the day – anyways.

31

This year Americade was to be different from the previous years. We decided we would make better use of our time and register for the full week. We entered various contest categories such as uniform competition and Queen of Americade.

There were only three of us brave enough to put our name on the dotted line and we certainly did not advertise our intentions. Of course, we were nervous! At our age we didn't know too many Grammas who were competing for Queen of anything.

To compete for the queen 'thing', there were interviews, an obstacle course and the uniform competition. The contests had some serious competitors. One of us dropped our bike in the obstacle course and another seemed to get lost on the course. My contribution, I rode the fastest-slow ride ever, Ha!

The interviews ran rather long. This year a larger number of women entered. Standing in the heat with no place to get out of the sun, some of us began to wonder if all this effort was really worth the aggravation. I for one said 'enough!' I left and was followed by the other two ladies. We were told later from 'someone in the know' there was a good chance we might have won because of our reputations as good riders. We would be a compliment to Americade but this time it wasn't meant to be. Aside from that day being especially warm, it was also the time of day we might have had a nap and these interviews were interfering with our rest. LOL

The uniform competition was a hoot and we did ourselves proud and brought home the President's Choice Award. One of the Judges asked if our being from all over was the reason for the discrepancy in uniform colour, WE said "Yes" of course. They didn't know that the uniform colour was always a big issue with the Club. What else could we say?

Another incident that made us laugh was when one of our Ladies had to remove a vest she was wearing underneath her uniform. With time being an issue, it was suggested that we as a group hold a flag around her and she could take the vest off. As she pulled the layers of clothes off, some of us joked about dropping the flag. You could see the look of concern in her eyes wondering if…as we started the countdown, one…two…three… No we didn't drop the flag…she wasn't sure and neither were we.

We were only a group of seven but when we entered the parade, to play down our small number, we chose not to decorate our bikes. We weren't grouped in with the other riders. No balloons, no stuffed animals, nothing was allowed on our bikes.

Our blue uniform top, grey slacks, white boots and white gloves made us unique from the various clubs riding around us. Lined along the parade route, voices from the crowds yelled, "Hey Motor Maids." It spoke volumes and we blossomed and our smiles spoke a thousand words.

Throughout the five day Rally we had a choice of activities available to us. Boat cruises, covered bridge rides, demo rides, a trip to Lake Placid and various rides throughout Vermont with scenery seen only in the Adirondacks and Green Mountains.

The night cruise on the main drag through Lake George isn't something to write home about, *except* during Americade. That's when four to five city blocks become a moving mass of thousands of bikes.

33

It can take an hour to ride this short distance from one end to the other.

The parade was of different name brand bikes. Some had a multitude of fantastic light systems flashing to the beat of music and the engines' roar. The muscle bikes are the complete atmosphere for some riders', and this is the place to see and the place to be seen.

Sometimes one or two of the bikes heat up and are pushed off the road. A fancy car may slither in but not for long (*wrong time-wrong place for him*). The sport bikes for a short distance may play games weaving in and out of traffic or popping wheelies amongst the bikes. The Police closely monitor the roads so it doesn't happen for long.

All of this we saw during the first week of June in Lake George. My friend left for home more relaxed and would be able to cope with the stress she knew would be waiting. We all felt revived and knew we would handle the everyday life we left behind for those few precious days.

Americade 2002 - we made a difference! The Motor Maids is the oldest Ladies riding club in North America but sometimes is thought to be the best-kept secret. Riders who know of us respect what our club stands for. We are not only the oldest; we are what we say we are – riders. Now after this year a few more will know of us and I believe sometimes less is best. That way we have quality members and not always does quantity count.

Motor Maids Org. founded in 1940…

Show Low Arizona 1995

Lights flashing, the unmarked police car led us back to the Curryville, MO Police Department. One more event we couldn't have predicted on this trip. Curryville, MO is a small town but infamous, so much so, it has been featured on the TV Show 20/20. They had the reputation of being one of the smallest towns in the U.S. with new police cars more often than most.

What was our reason for following him? We were clocked doing 53mph in a 35mph zone. I would want to dispute the numbers. I was tail rider of a five-bike group and I KNOW I was not going that fast but…when on vacation sometimes it's best to just pay and move on.

There must have been a couple of moments when we all had a grin on our faces though. We and the police car followed/chased our lead rider who was taking just a little longer to pull over. She did say later that she wasn't going to pull over in the gravel for anyone and we knew that.

When we all finally stopped he checked all the ownerships, held on to our licenses and asked us to follow him. *We had a choice?* The most embarrassing part was all five of us following him into town with his lights still flashing. I'm sure some of the locals (early morning – 7am) might have thought, 'here come some more.' Imagine; five fines at one time! Good timing! *Bah Humbug!*

This trip would not be soon forgotten by any of us, for different reasons. For the first time in my riding career I was riding a sport-touring bike, the Honda ST1100. This was her first long distance ride and I should have known better. The riding difference between the ST and my Wing was the most difficult to deal with but I *really, really* wanted this bike and I got her. Oops!!! *Watch what you wish for.*

She was a Beauty. Black, fast, maneuverable, large gas tank (7 gallons opposed to the 5 on my Wings) and large hard bags for storage. As much as I loved the bike, my body complained from the time I got on her until I got off. My wrists tingled constantly and standing up was the only way to give some relief to my curled legs. I will never forget the miles of ribbon highway through New Mexico in that prone position. Not good at the best of times when riding any motorcycle.

Show Low too left many sad memories. This Convention was not supposed to be on my list in 1995 due to a previously planned trip to Europe in the fall. My Florida companion had decided not to attend too but at the last minute we both changed our minds so we could show each other our new ST's.

Registration at the Hotel was fairly quiet that day and this was strange. I found out why. I was taken aside and informed that my friend had been killed in a car/bike accident en route to Convention. The shock felt as though someone had kicked me in the stomach. I didn't want to believe for those short moments that what I was hearing was true.

36

My friend and her traveling companion were riding through Mississippi in that early morning and she was hit head-on by an oncoming car traveling over the rise of a hill in her lane. The driver had fallen asleep after a long nights work.

Those are the times I want my husband near and hearing his voice on the phone helped to calm me enough to deal with this sadness. Those in charge had called my home to inform me of the accident but I had already left for Show Low. Frank was prepared for my inevitable phone call.

At that same Convention a second Motor Maid was tragically killed stepping off the curb in front of the Hotel and was hit by an oncoming vehicle. The shock of losing two well known and admired members painted that year with a very dark shade of gray.

The loss of my dear friend, an uncomfortable ride and that blasted ticket was a time never meant to be, and never forgotten.

A farewell letter to my friend, Nancy

We never dreamed our trip in 1994 would be our final travel together, but we did it right. Together we climbed one of the highest mountains in the World and soared down like eagles on steel wings. Only another rider would understand the high it gave us, and we did it together. Thank you Nancy for the good times even though they were much too short. I'll miss you forever and forget you – never.

37

Chico California 2003

The road to Chico California was long, taking 4 weeks and 3 days before we were all safely home and back to what each of us called 'our life.'

There were six of us on this Motor Maid Convention-bound ride. We all had a number of miles under our belts and had traveled together numerous times so our riding positions and comfort level was good. We were an awesome sight! Our bikes were top of the line including two Yamaha V-Stars, two Harley touring bikes, one Kawasaki Voyager pulling a Bushtec trailer and mine, a Honda Gold Wing. Our group included four grandmothers, one great grandmother and a youngster not quite 50. I must mention that one of our ladies had just had her last chemo treatment and nothing was going to keep her from this trip. Nothing!

Six motorcycles traveling together generated a lot of curiosity from drivers and perhaps some congestion in traffic so we tried to be aware of any vehicles around us. With the help of three CB's, when traffic backed up or someone wanted to pass us we would move over to single file. Then back to staggered formation after the vehicle had safely passed us.

One incident told us that no matter how careful we were, there was always something we couldn't anticipate...

It was hot and dry that day while riding on a fairly flat stretch through the desert lands. With the rolling expanse of hills around us, there were times you could literally see miles ahead of you. A pickup truck started to pass so we routinely moved over and watched as it overtook each bike. The mini-seconds slowly ticked as he passed each bike. When he was finally beside the lead bike, it was as though he'd forgotten what he was doing. With the unusual time he was taking to pass me (the lead), I was apprehensive. "What was he doing?" "Why was he taking so long?" Someone could be coming toward us!

Ahead of us an oncoming vehicle was flashing its lights… then again… A split second later, the last thing I remember seeing was a spray of gravel and the car fighting to get back up on the pavement. In the meantime the pickup driver woke up and disappeared. No one was hurt but all six of us couldn't believe what had almost happened. I know the words out of my mouth were not printable. In doing the right thing we realized then, there are some drivers you can't think for. Maybe, they can't think for themselves, either. It can be dangerous out there.

The air was hot and sticky the day we stopped to shop in St. Cloud Minnesota. Once we were finished we headed out of town to the highways, hoping the movement of the bikes might cool us down. That day was relatively promising but as the hours passed we started to see and feel the difference, temperatures and distance can make. The weather was constantly changing. Light rain, wind and then black clouds hovering over us so low, you felt you could reach up and touch them. The rain again came back with a vengeance. We had gone a number of miles further before we would see a promise of sunshine on the far horizon. Fields were filled with water and flooding ditches that spread on to the roads. At that moment we didn't know we had wandered onto Tornado Alley (our name) that hot day in June. Later we would witness the aftermath of a twister.

Parker Minnesota, once a thriving little town; was a scene of confusion. Disheveled torn up trees, vacant land that was once a baseball stadium

39

and towns people redirecting the traffic through and around downed trees. This day was the most devastating to all of us but luckily we were unscathed once again. We later found out there had been 50 sited twister touchdowns around us that day.

As we continued on, our plans included the Black Hills, Mount Rushmore and especially black hills gold for some. Yellowstone was to be a three day stop and for me the Wild Life Highway. There were so many animals and the beauty of nature was all around us to capture on film.

While staying in the Xanterra Lodges in Yellowstone early one morning we heard a commotion outside. I wandered out to see what it was all about. I noticed a group of people standing across the road. Their attention was turned to one of the lodges where two Elk were resting or sleeping on a grassy knoll behind it. I took some pictures; retreated back to our cottage only to be called out again by my friend when she hollered, "bring your camera!"

Meandering down a path in front of our lodges we witnessed a large number of buffalo heading toward us on a slow quest to somewhere. They were so close to the bikes that we crossed our fingers they weren't curious about all that chrome. The bikes didn't seem to exist to them as they made their way past and out of our area. Whew!!!!

Later we were told that one of the Elk had used the aerial of one of the Harleys, as dental floss? I was told this Harley lacked for nothing but dental floss? Right! I guess that could be a compliment to whomever. Huh?

It took us 12 days to finally arrive in steamy Chico. We said our 'how are you?' and "what's been happening?" and the Convention settled down to the reason we were there in the first place.

One of the most prized awards for a district is the 'most accumulated mileage' pin to Convention and Eastern Canada won again! Hooray for us! California is a long way to travel for a charm but this one is worth it, for some. The Motor Maids are a riding club and that means you must ride your bike no matter where the Convention is held. You cannot trailer or ride double up or you will have no voting privileges in the meetings.

During free time, a bus trip was planned by the host district, to shop and sightsee in San Francisco. Along the Bay the temperatures dramatically changed from the high 90's in Chico to the low 60's. It was a relief for this Canadian girl. I do not deal well with extreme heat so I was much more comfortable for a few hours.

All too soon Convention was over. Our six Ladies said their goodbyes one more time to our friends as well as to two of our road companions. Due to the heat I decided I would go north instead of south towards Las Vegas. To go north meant it had to cool down, right?

One girl opted to go home by way of Bakersfield Calif. while another headed south to Florida. We had agreed earlier in the trip that if the route changed it would not be a problem. The weather had to cool down!

Now we were four, heading north to Crater Lake Oregon, the remains of Mount Mazama. This mountain erupted hundreds of years ago creating a crystal blue coloured lake. It is considered to be the deepest

41

Lake in the United States as well as Holy Ground to the Klamath Indians. The lake boasts to be at its deepest point, 1943 feet deep.

On the same route we visited Sisters, OR and the Lava Grounds around the Twin Sisters Mountains. The landscape is reminiscence of what the face of the moon might look like but this land had skeletons of trees highlighting the blackness of the rocks.

In July, the west was plagued with forest fires. Luckily, we didn't encounter one but our route was changed slightly because of the possibility of smoke and pass closures.

We were advised to take another route that might be a wee bit curvy. The alternate route put all our skills to the ultimate test. Curves turned into twisty hairpin turns, U-turns, turns in gravel, etc. etc. etc. You name it, we rode it but oh the scenery! We would never have seen it otherwise. The forest was thick with stunted trees and jagged rocks. The colour misty green came to mind, almost surreal and pristine to the eye. It was a picture waiting to be taken.

Continuing north we stayed in Golden British Columbia. In the morning a Gondola ride up Kicking Horse Pass was a must for one and an endurance test for another. I love heights and one Motor Maid did not. She is also one of my dearest friends and tolerated just one more of my wishes. Once we rode to the top of the mountain she refused to wander outside the restaurant to look out at the mountains. We had *only* gone 11,266 ft up the mountain! Now that is a true friend.

 Lake Louise was beautiful of course. My last visit was in 1986 on my way to Yakima Washington. Not much has changed except a newer, bigger Hotel was being built and there were more people.

I Did You Can Too

At Kenora Ontario our group split up one more time, two of us headed southeast to Ohio and two, east towards Peterborough. After a long days' ride and one more night on the road, my friend and I parked our bikes in her driveway in Vermilion.

All of us had so many stories to tell to those who would listen. Some of us took more pictures than others. North America is so beautiful that you could only appreciate it from a motorcycle. We had also ridden a part of one of the largest mountain ranges in the world.

We each totaled over 7650 miles plus and it was agreed if asked, would we do it again?

You bet, in a heartbeat. Life is short. Live it, ride it.

The cost of a lifetime:

Six Motor Maids headed to Chico California - a dream come true
Cost - five weeks of time

Compatibility on the road –best most of the time
Cost – generosity and loyalty

Experiences to share with Grandchildren – memorable
Cost – Desire

Weather changes – dealt with
Cost – change of one motel

Friendships after five weeks – continued
Cost – pride

Time of our lives –
 Cost -PRICELESS

Cherokee, NC

Our destination that year was Cherokee, NC. It was especially anticipated by many for its reputation of great riding roads including the Blue Ridge Parkway in the Smoky Mountains.

One stretch of highway in the Mountains is called the 'tail of the dragon.' The route starts at Deals Gap, NC, and runs 11 miles to Tennessee. It can be a test for the novice and experienced riders with 318 twists and turns. The names of some of the turns include *'Crossroads of time, The Hump, Horns of the dragon, The Slide, Hog pen bend'* and at the end of the road, *'The Pearly Gates.' Ominous names for ominous roads!*

That year we could never have known what lay ahead for some girls. Circumstances beyond their control prevented them from fulfilling the thrill of a lifetime due to senseless accidents and a tornado. The storm blacked out a one hundred mile radius along our route to just a few hundred feet from some of our Hotels' front doors. One more time we had wandered onto Tornado Alley.

For a 24 hour period as we rode to Convention, we experienced the constant changes of torrential rain, wind, sun then wind again. We felt a bad omen all around us.

Some riders were stopped by toppled trees and warned by police and locals to get off the Parkway. At one point, with one huge tree lying in their path there was no choice. An awful accident occurred just ahead of us (not our ladies) involving a Harley Group. It was gut wrenching seeing four full dressed motorcycles lying on the side of the mountain.

I don't deal well with accidents so I pulled off the Parkway to calm down. We were a group of four and as we changed into dryer clothes (it's pouring of course) another group of our riders from Canada joined us. They informed us one of our girls had been involved in a senseless accident the day before.

After a long thirteen hour ride to the Convention site we watched, concerned for some of our members. Late in the evening, uninjured they rode into their hotel parking lot, a hotel with no power.

One girl lost control of her sport bike on the Dragon's Tail and had a badly injured chest and shoulder. Another, traveling on a different route lost control when her front tire rode over the tail of a snake and crashed into the guardrail. Two Canadian girls were air lifted back home to Canada for months of rehab while a Florida girl bandaged and sedated, stayed at the hotel until the Convention was over.

Personally, (not related to the weather) I almost lost control of 'Ghost' while pulling a new trailer, traveling faster than the trailer would allow. This would be solved, for the first time in my riding career I WOULD see every flower and twig on the side of the road. Once I hit a certain speed the trailer would go into a wobble shaking the bike all over the road. Reality check for me on this trip was to 'slow down!'

Our Convention this year certainly took on a different meaning for some. The renewing of friendships is most important. For some it's all about the ride and there are some journeys that you just never forget. Cherokee was one of them.

Old World – New Testaments

White Lining ....

Now, depending on the continent you're traveling, rules of the road can be different. Motorcycling in North America has been around for a good number of years but compared to other countries it has almost always been a second choice. Compared to America, highways overseas were very congested. The high cost of petrol means smaller sized motorcycles were more acceptable and affordable. The vehicular world accepted the bikes more as transportation on or off the main highways. Motorcyclists too are more readily accepted having some of the same rights as a four wheeled vehicle.

Many people have heard of the Autobahn in Europe and the Autostrada in Italy. They are awestruck with the reported reputation of high speeds. I have traveled on both, as well as most major highways in America. I find the European roads to be more organized and drivers know what to expect because in most cases, rules seem to be obeyed.

My Rules of Thumb are very simple.

On the Autobahn, you do not pass in the slow lane (it is meant for slow moving trucks, buses etc). When you want to pass – your place is the center lane but if you want to fly – move into the passing lane. Once in this lane, if you see what appears to be the faintest glimmer of candle lights coming up behind you, "Get out of the way!" or you'll be run over. A phrase comes to mind from the movie Star Wars, "there is always a bigger fish" or in this case a faster car.

47

A new term/action I learned in Europe was filtering, lane splitting or white lining. Again knowing the rules of the roads, these actions can certainly change your progress when traffic begins to back up or just slow down.

White lining means exactly that, traveling on the white line between stalled vehicles and with caution carefully proceeding ahead. The freedom is, knowing that drivers will allow you as a biker to pass their stalled vehicle on that white line as long as you are careful and don't abuse the privilege. Bikes have the agility and size to pass and there is nothing more intolerable to a rider, then to follow a truck spewing diesel fumes as you wait for the traffic to resume its speed.

One time, the fumes were so sickening, my companion said while passing a truck I literally disappeared for a brief second or two. There are days now, the smell of diesel fumes bring back reminders of certain parts of Germany to me.

Here in America, white lining is FORBIDDEN! Allowing a bike to move to the front of stalled cars is generally NOT allowed, and passing in the slow lane seems to be the NORM. What is wrong with this picture?

We, in America, have great Interstates and wonderful roads. The feeling is once you get on them, it's a race and rules don't apply unless a police car is visible. There are times some drivers don't seem to know what lane they should be in or the car ahead must be passed. These roads are ideal to get quickly from point A to point B. If given a choice, I prefer the secondary highways. That way I can appreciate the country around me and can stop and 'smell the roses' or fields freshly peppered with *manure* and even the strong scent of garlic. Life is so fast. Why make it faster when you can take an easier route and enjoy one more ride…*and this according to the 'Ghost'…*

48

Graves 1990

This motorcycle trip was my very first to Europe and there were times I felt I had stepped into another period in time. Row upon row they stand nestled in a misty forest in Holten, Holland. White grave markers and crosses mark their final resting place of so many years ago. These were also the graves of the young and brave brothers of two of my companions.

Quite often I will visit gravesites while traveling and this year was no different. Our visit was to Holten and then to Nijmegan, Groesbeek Canadian War Memorial in the Netherlands. It wasn't difficult to feel the over powering sadness there.

Until we planned this trip, I didn't know the history of our companions' family, and their losses. I learned that the couple had each lost a brother in World War 2 and my lady friend spoke of being especially close to her brother. As a young girl, she remembered waiting for word of her brother coming home safely. Her families' hopes and dreams being dashed with an unwelcome knock on her parent's door. Now for the first time in over fifty years she would lay eyes on his grave.

Gratitude to Canada's support during wartime has been shown to the world in Europe by the erection of War Memorials. Dieppe France, Bergen-op-Zoom, the Royal Winnipeg Rifles, near Courseulles-sur-mer and Juno Beach are but a few. There have been so many young men who died leaving behind so much sadness.

49

Between the crosses, row on row,
That mark our place: and in the sky
The Larks, still bravely singing, fly.
We are the Dead.
Short days ago
We lived, felt dawn, saw sunset glow,
Loved and were loved, and now we lie
In Flanders Field…
Written by John McCrae 1915   WW1

History has a voice and can be seen in books, stories, TV *and* on the engravings of a stone. It is so sad that someone can live such a vital life and then in the end they are just a name and date. More often now when a detail is revealed on the marker suddenly that person speaks.

I had always thought of Alexander Graham Bell, assistant/inventor of the telephone, as a Canadian. Reading his tombstone, he was an American citizen buried in a Canadian Graveyard in Baddeck Nova Scotia. This was his statement to the world for those who cared.

Imagine two little girls holding hands. They are approximately seven and ten years old with ribbon tied pigtails and lace edged socks. The collars on their dresses also have crocheted pineapples on them. Now imagine them standing as life size bronze statues on their own grave. I saw these little girls in Athens Ohio while attending a Women's Motorcycle Conference in the year 2000. The epitaph said very little but the girl's statue alone told much of their story. They were too young to die.

Many stories have been told of a young Maiden in France who spoke to the Angels at the age of 13 until she was burned at the stake at the age of 19. To walk in the home of Joan of Arc, born in, Domrémy la

Pucelle (near Rouen France), was humbling. Joan's ashes were tossed into the Seine River but in 1920 Pope Benedict XV canonized Joan and her memory will live on, *without* an official burial site. Visiting Joan's home and attending a French service at the Carmelite Church told me this was a special place. I had lost a child that year and the Church helped me to understand things I had not until that day... there are reasons for everything.

In a little town in Ontario named Port Colborne, an engraved headstone says it all. Detail is especially spectacular showing a man and women walking hand in hand into the sunset with two Harley Davidson Motorcycles flanking either side of them. Such workmanship will be admired for years to come. I have heard these fine etchings will not stand the test of time as long as the old. Pollution in our air now will destroy them much sooner.

The Dom Cathedral in Cologne Germany boasts of housing the Reliquary (casket) of the Three Wise Men (Magi). The Shrine is a large gilded and decorated triple Sarcophagus and is placed above and behind the High Alter of the Cathedral. It boasts the largest Reliquary in the World, and is also the largest Gothic Church in Northern Europe. The master goldsmith in the 12th / 13th century; brought the remains of the Three Kings to Cologne from Milan and were interred at this church. The building of the church started in 1248AD, survived the Wars and finally-*almost* –completed in the 19th Century.

The Cathedral was the first and largest I had ever been in. I remember walking down cement steps into the basement of the Church. The temps were cool. It felt damp and claustrophobic. (*I was the only one of our group that went in that direction – maybe less people?*) I then exited the basement and wandered to the main entrance where everyone had gathered. The centre of the church was so big and elegant and too *noisy*

51

for a church. There were sounds of chairs being dragged across marble floors, practicing organ music, camera flashes and different groups of *so* many people. It wasn't hard to get lost in the crowd. I did the touristy thing, took my pictures and then retraced my steps out to the courtyard where food vendors were busy with the lunchtime crowd. My friends and I ate lunch at a local McDonalds that day. For a split second I was overwhelmed by where I was. Standing in the courtyard below the church entrance I pirouetted in a semi-circle. Canadian flag in one hand, a coffee in the other then spun around on one foot as a flock of pigeons flew away from me. One of my companions took a picture of that moment I treasure today.

Perched on the side of a mountain in Austria along the Hallstatter See is the quaint little town of Hallstatt. It also has the distinction of having one- way traffic, with one signal light at each end of town. Only one car at a time can enter or exit Hallstatt – one road east to west.

There is also a 16th Century Gothic Church possessing 15th century paintings and a charnel house. Due to the lack of burial space for the dead, a custom was created that is *-unusual.* For many centuries the custom was to unearth the bones after 12 to 15 years. Leave them in the sun to dry and then paint them. The men's skulls might be painted with an Ivy-Oak design and the women's with Alpine flowers. The names, date of death and reason of death were also included.

In 1970 the church eventually allowed the cremation of the skulls. They are now a tourist attraction and have been featured in National Geographic magazine. Outside of this Charnel house is an above ground children's graveyard. The graves say it all. It was too soon…

Ferries

Many times our trips took us to parts of the European world that were only accessible by the use of Ferries. Having a ferry as an option, air lifting our bikes made no sense and could be expensive plus time consuming. Our trips included the use of various sized boats and ports of entry.

Names of a few of the ports include Holyhead GB to Dublin Ireland, Rosslare Ireland to Wales, Dover to Calais FR. and Newcastle UK to Bergen Norway. My preference at all times would be the shorter trips.

Smaller crossings would take us across the Rhine at Assmanhaussen in just minutes. In a few hours we could be in Fishguard Wales by way of Rosslare Ireland. Newcastle GB would be an overnight trip taking us to Stavanger Norway.

Each ship has a different entrance for motorcycles depending on the real purpose of the ship. Some are meant mainly for the transfer of human cargo and small vehicles. Others are large enough to transfer train cars and 18 wheel transport trucks.

The vessel accepting a train also has tracks that can be dangerous for bikes. Smaller boats carrying nothing larger than cars and small trucks may have a metal rail / ramp leading up the side of the boat. This can be dangerous too if it's wet. (*One ramp was so steep if I would have seen it before hand I might have changed my mind.*)

The loading surface can be a nightmare for riders and Stewards. The stewards are experienced in more than just directing traffic. I have seen Stewards walking bikes aboard or down and off the ship, if a rider has a problem. They also help those who might not know the proper way to tie their bike down. I haven't seen too many riders who didn't know how to do this. I have asked for assistance with the knots that are used to secure the bikes. We don't want our bikes damaged and the last thing a Steward needs is a bike loose and tossed around on choppy seas.

The largest ship (Stena Lines) took us from Newcastle UK to Bergen Norway, and might have been described as a moving Mall. It had the amenities of a few city blocks and three different restaurants from McDonalds to Haute Cuisine with service that lacked for nothing. There were a couple of bars/dance floors, liquor stores, theatres, exquisite gift shoppes, corner stores, the Money Exchange and rooms for children to watch and play video games. Human size cartoon figures walk amongst the children, entertaining them in various ways. One child though was traumatized by a cartoon character and taken to a quiet spot to settle down. *All cartoons are not funny to all children.*

One room that interested us on this trip was the 'quiet room.' Generally, families with children would not use this room plus you had to pay extra for a separate key to enter. The room provided lounge chairs and couches, newspapers, smoking areas, free coffee, tea, snacks and fruit. This room was locked away from the bustle of crowded noisy walkways. The 'quiet' room would be a must the next time we traveled on this ship.

For this overnight trip to Bergen Norway we reserved a small berth so we would be rested for our ride into Norway.

A small berth might infer there would be more space rather than trying to rest on deck. It did if you walked in and backed out. For the short time we were on the boat, we found it to be sufficient. The berth had one set of bunks, just 60" long (I'm 5'11"). A small shower stall and toilet in the same cubicle plus a sink and wardrobe across from it rounded out the space. Real close quarters but we weren't going to live there, just rest for a while and it *was* quiet.

In the morning, the ship comes alive with passengers crowding the walkways anxious to get to their cars and bikes. The atmosphere is a bit chaotic but seems to be reasonably controlled. One important number to remember is your deck number. Without it you could be wandering for days looking for your vehicle. The traffic would have a problem moving if you were parked in the middle. Bikes are usually put in a tight corner or along the sides of the ship. Last vehicle on the ship usually means first off. We were usually last to board.

Anticipation builds as you wait for the boats' nose to open up. There is an excitement you feel when you ride up the ramp and on to the freedom of the road. Interest in the bikes is visible. I'm sure there were many watching and wishing they were riding the bikes instead of a 4 wheeled cage. *When it's raining,* I know exactly how I would feel.

Le Havre and Dieppe 2000

All my life, I've had concerns of being locked in an elevator, public washrooms and long corridors. I have handled the what-ifs. I guess you might call it a minor type of claustrophobia but the problem never reared its ugly head until a day in Le Havre France as we were waiting for our Ferry back to the UK.

The Hotel in Le Havre was full when we arrived. My companion and I were each assigned separate rooms in a school dormitory adjacent to the hotel. The tiny rooms had all the amenities a foreign student would need when away from home while attending school or working on the Cruise Ship Lines. The time of year was considered off – season so most of the rooms in the dormitory were empty having a skeletal staff on duty maintaining the building.

My room was two stories higher then my companions. For reasons of my own and at my request, my companion and I carried my mattress down to her room and the two of us shared her room. The maintenance man observed our antics in the elevator transferring the mattress but made no comment.

We stayed at the hotel's dorm two days and while we waited we toured the city of Le Havre with plans to go to Dieppe during our stay. That day we were headed to the Canadian War Memorial in Dieppe. While exiting the elevator to the underground Parking, it was strange that the garage door was partially down.

We loaded our bikes and drove to the entrance and pushed the green button but nothing could move it. We both got off the bikes and again,

56

pushed the buttons and hollered for anyone who might hear us but no one did. We then tried to think of other ways to get the door opened.

My friend retreated back up the staircase to the entrance to see if anyone could help and found the door locked too. In the meantime I had been doing anything I could to make the door move. By this point I was anxious and not having any mechanical or electrical talents it was like the blind leading the blind. Pushing buttons did nothing and no one could be seen. The door's mechanism looked simple enough. It was held in place by a coiled spring hanging at an odd angle but not attached to anything. When all else fails why not try to muscle the door up? I was able to push the door up until it was high enough to get the bikes out. It was that simple!

I rode my bike out and called to my friend to get hers out fast. We didn't know if the door would get jammed again. We rode up the underground ramp and a few minutes later we were finally able to continue with our plans to tour Dieppe.

This fear I have of being locked in, is always present. Until something happens, I don't know what I'll do but hopefully with a cool head and some patience the situation will change. I deal with it. Luckily there haven't been many times and maybe I wasn't the only one concerned?

Venice 2000

The year of the Millennium Celebrations in France opened one more door. Ten years after getting my motorcycle license, I was now comfortable traveling to international cities that I at one time had only heard of. During my years of traveling in Europe I belonged to the International Motorcycle Touring Club. The membership provided a wealth of information for the necessities to travel on foreign soil. The IMTC was comparable to the Motor Maids. The only difference was the continent. Riding anywhere in the world was possible with their valued assistance.

Members of the IMTC in England assisted in many ways. Individually or as a group they would meet us in Airports and drive us to bike Rentals. Some provided meals and a night's rest at their homes or arranged for lodgings near the rental in various cities. Many members would also ride with us through horrendous traffic in some cities. *London can be crazy even during the off times!* One member graciously allowed me to leave my bike at his home for a couple of years between trips. I could never thank them enough for their generosity and expertise, I am honoured to call them friends and we are still in touch this many years later.

The celebration of the Millennium in France brought forward members from all over the world. A good number of the riders lived in England and they were my closest contacts when assistance was needed.

My companion and I decided that after the celebration in France 2000 we were close enough to see Italy and especially Venice. Various Club members had traveled extensively throughout Italy and when asking for some 'wee words of wisdom' we were helped in many ways.

It was suggested that we find a city with a train station, one hour outside of Venice. Leaving our bikes at our Hotel and taking a train into Venice eliminated parking problems. It would also allow us the freedom and energy to tour Venice all day and not worry about traveling at night on unknown Roads. My friend and I still have vivid memories of our night ride in the mountains to Clausthal-Zellerfeld Germany - ten years earlier. NOT A FUN TIME!

Honda 440 - Courier bikes

It was a mistake (but not) to rent these bikes. We were so used to riding our 1320 Harley and 1500 Gold Wing touring bikes in America, these 440's felt like kid's toys and being the spoiled riders we were, it was very difficult to say that it wasn't a problem. To be honest they did save our butts though when we ran into new roadway construction and a detour on our mountain ride through the Swiss Alps.

If we would have been riding our touring bikes, maneuvering them over fist size rocks used on the newly graded road would have been almost impossible. The blessing that day - these bikes were small enough we could manhandle them .Sounds of the little motors revving spoke volumes as we tiptoed through the rocks and onto a newly paved roadway. When we were finally on our way, I said a silent prayer to one of my angels.

Money is always an issue so that year we'd decided we would rent Hondas. They would be the smallest bikes yet and we thought 'why not'? Near the end of the trip the riding was so uncomfortable we chose to walk or ride trains from Walton on the Thames to London waiting for our date of departure. Once the bikes were parked at the last B&B, my friend announced that she "WOULD NOT SIT ON **that** BIKE ONE SECOND LONGER!" until the moment we had to take them back to the rental. She was determined and we really *are* oh so spoiled.

Postcards of Venice pale in comparison when you walk over the bridges spanning the canals in Venice. I remember the day being especially hot but the atmosphere in the city gave off an ambiance of being one of the special cities that I would always remember. We did the usual touristy thing with souvenirs, photos and when visiting Venice, a ride in a Gondola was a must. Of course we expected that he would sing for us but when asked, he announced "I don't sing." They did it in the movies! He didn't sing? Imagine! Hmm, but he *could* talk. In spite of his broken English I *almost* understood parts of his dialogue of local interests when he slowed down and pointed at them. All in all though, it was a fun day.

Venice at the best of times is busy but this day with the steamy heat it was a relief just to stand in the shade looking down on the canal boats. There were people everywhere including the top of St. Marks Basilica. My thoughts at the time, it was a sacrilege for people to be up there. We also rode Venice's waterways in a motorized boat. Every type of vessel could be seen at any given time. I saw huge ships with crates of tropical flowers, too many tour boats, a wedding boat, many private 'cigar' boats and even a police patrol boat.

There are many places I would want to see again. Venice's canals hold a fascination for me and for that reason I would want to come back. Venice also runs a close second to Delft Holland another favourite of mine. *I can't get enough of those canals.*

On our return trip to England we visited a few other famous cities of the World including London, Paris and Geneva. Although interesting to visit they are very much alike to me and it would take a life time to see it all. One of my dreams is to spend 48 hours in the centre of these famous cities, rise early the first day, wander the streets for good photos and retire until early dusk for the night shots. Even though I haven't had my perfect 48, I still have my memories and I am so very fortunate.

The day I received the key to my motorcycle, a new world opened up and who would have ever thought one day I would be riding in a Venetian gondola asking the Gondolier to sing for us? Certainly not me…

Holland 2001

40 some years ago these canal roads must have seemed so different. The atmosphere now is not like what she left behind as a young child when she migrated to Canada. She left behind memories coloured by World War 2. As much as she was enjoying her visit to Dordrecht, she commented that 'we' in a free society have no idea what life was like until you lived 'it.' Her bitter words were, 'War is Hell on Earth' and she knew, she had been there. There were so many sad times and memories for her. She would experience the difference by coming back to visit her hometown one more time, remembering some of the early days as a child, a lifetime ago.

Traveling with those who lived in Europe during wartime, to go back and see through adult eyes what she remembered is reason enough to be there. Clinging to the memories of the past, oft times moulds us to the person we are today, good or bad. In her case she was able to bring back the good ones as she took us on a tour of Dordrecht Holland. She discovered that not much had really changed. The home she had grown up in was still intact and occupied, her church and school was now a nursery school and the ditches she played and skated on only seemed deeper. Other than that everything appeared almost, as she remembered it. *What I remember the most of that visit was the number of ditches and the bridges. Lots of bridges!*

Holland, meaning hollow land, is known for its canals and windmills. Riding and enjoying the countryside from a motorcycle was an added pleasure. Small town activities were ongoing in communities as we passed through. Activities included swim marathons in the muddy canal waters, costume balls and festivals of all kinds. Property decorations were comparable to ours on various months in Canada.

Holland is wonderfully clean and has so much history. We had
unknowingly wandered into the celebrations of the 375th year
anniversary of the retrieval of land from the sea.

I later learned through books and the internet that this reclaimed land
had been one of the designated sites by U.N.E.S.C.O (United Nations
Educational Scientific & Cultural Organization). It is called the
Beemster Polder, dated from the 17th Century and is the oldest area of
reclaimed land in the Netherlands. In retrieving their land, the Dutch
People have preserved intact, well-ordered landscapes of fields, canal,
dykes and settlements laid out in accordance with the Classical and
Renaissance planning principals. This achievement is unique not to be
found anywhere else in the world. It has been compared to the Great
Wall of China and the Pyramids in Egypt.

Later that day, our travels took us to the mini-metropolis of Delft, built
along another web of canals, that were easy to explore by foot, bike
and boat. Delft is an intimate, attractive traditional city. It is famous for
its' blue/white earthenware seen all over the world in china shoppes.

We later visited the city of The Hague along the North Sea, famous for
the beach itself and of course the Peace Palace. It is a powerful world
diplomatic capital and the seat of government for the Netherlands. In
the near future, war criminal Vladimir Milosevic would be tried for war
crimes against humanity at the Palace. He was at present being housed
in a nearby jail until his day in Court.

One more stop that day was to be to Madurodam, a miniature Holland
duplicated to the scale of 1/52 of its life size. The weather was taking a
turn for the worse so we cut our trip short and headed back to our
B&B in Delft.

While my friend and I traveled, our third companion was taking a day off to rest in Delft and found a quaint restaurant specializing in Sea Foods - *of course*. That night the three of us indulged in the wonderful food this fine city had to offer.

When riding a motorcycle you DO meet some of the nicest people. The day we were headed for The Hague we routinely pulled our bikes over to the side of the Highway just to check our maps. A young man on a Sport Bike stopped to ask if we needed assistance. My friend spoke Dutch and said we weren't lost, just checking our maps. He asked if we'd like to get off the highways and see a nicer part of the country. He was headed home after work at the Schiphol Airport. We were so pleased and said, "Yes we would." We would see so much more of "The Holland" we wanted to see instead of playing highway chess on this major road.

We followed his bike through traffic apparently looking for quieter roads, but then the traffic came to a halt. We filtered through the stalled cars to the front of the lineup and were informed there had been a bad accident in the tunnel ahead of us. Our guide spoke to the Officer in charge. We were directed to a recently cut opening in an Industrial Park fence eventually leading us onto local roads. We took a short ferry ride and then on to quieter, picturesque streets. This is what postcards are made of.

He led us past fully functioning authentic windmills, not one but a row of maybe a dozen. Passing a country fair we opted out to see the countryside. While stopped he fiddled with my headlight which at the best of times was not working properly. It really wasn't a problem traveling during the day's light. After an hour or so we eventually separated, said our goodbyes and he turned to go home. Before we parted company I offered his three children Canadian pins that I carry

64

with me for that reason and he was pleased. I'm sure our time together was one of his slower rides home. He chose that moment to slow down and share the last part of it with us. We were so fortunate to have met this local rider. Through his generosity, we experienced Holland differently than we would have seen from the highway. It is true that some of the nicest people are riding motorcycles.

Czechoslovakia 1992

Eastern Europe in the early nineties was a time of transition for everyone, residents and visitors alike. Each country had many government problems that divided the individual states into separate countries. Such as Czechoslovakia becoming Czech and Slovakia.

For some in our group, we couldn't imagine living through the day to day turmoil that these countries and people suffered. As North American riders, used to riding fairly large new motorcycles, some locals saw the opulence our rented toys represented and resented our presence.

Arriving at pre-booked hotels, attention was always diverted to the bikes and us. We were women! Americans! Actually we were Canadians and one American rider so on later trips we would wear something that showed what country we did come from. *Various countries tolerated Canadians and Americans for different reasons. We were always aware when crossing borders, the country that was preferred. The length of time the customs held onto your passport, spoke volumes and they sure liked to hold onto ours so much longer.*

We knew of this because one of our girls was American and she passed through customs most time in a heartbeat. Not the Canadians. This was not a good sign. One comment on our trip from a Canadian was that Joe Clarke Canadian ambassador/foreign minister had best get busy and do a better job representing Canada.

Our pre-arranged lodgings were always more than acceptable. That was one more preference my Club in the UK in time would understand. We didn't need five star hotels; we only requested clean rooms and good food. North America has a bad reputation for accepting nothing other than what opulence allows. They really didn't know us until this trip. (*This was the first trip Sandra Clark (former MM) and Jim Kentish, I.M.T.C. planned for the Motor Maids*)

The safety of our bikes was monumental to our continued travels. Parking them might be underground or at fenced- in compounds with armed security officers monitoring them throughout the nights. It was thought for some, out of sight meant out of mind. Not so for one couple. Their two BMW's complete tail light systems were stripped from their bikes at the entrance to our Hotel on a bright sunny afternoon. (*Once again… the local Gypsies were blamed*)

Our daily travels took us on back roads rather than major highways. We could see the difference we 'Americans' assumed might be normal. Naively, I/we were surprised to see some farms still being operated by the young and old. Women in their late70's – 80's were hand tying wheat sheaves in triangular shapes leaving them in straight rows in the fields for future use. Men worked the horse drawn wagons on semi-paved roads. None smiled as we passed each other. In fact some resented our very presence, occasionally showing their fists at us.

As a child my parents' pictures of the 1920's to 1940's in Canada were reminiscent of what we saw those days.

This country gave me an un-wanted look into a past I was too young to understand and this was the 90's.

There were many reasons for turmoil during this transition bringing more stressful times to an already burdened country. With support from the Party, huge farms thrived having money for new equipment to operate their farms. Once the Party had withdrawn, many of the

67

farms were abandoned. Again the people were damned if they did and damned if they didn't.

Now riding through the back roads of this country we were witness to the aftermath of previously cultivated groomed fields abandoned and left to grow wild again. Cattle barns had no enclosures surrounding them and no equipment was visible except un-useable pieces, abandoned in the fields. All the work farmers had laboriously completed during their farm years was gone, allowing nature to reclaim the land -once again.

We'd entered another time period when we crossed through the fallen Berlin Wall. The West had freedom. With that came prosperity and a more contented people. The East was the opposite. Checkpoint Charlie as the 'wall' was called; prevented those in the east to live in the west and many were killed in failed attempts to leave. Eventually the 'wall' did come down but circumstances didn't change overnight. It is still taking many years to change those eyes. It never ceases to amaze me that no matter how devastated a city or village was, there was always a church.

Faith remained strong and sometimes it was the only thread left to hang on to.

Dachau & Auschwitz – Reality Check 1994

The artificially lit cubicles were similar to schools I had attended during my youth. These rooms spoke of a horror I couldn't have imagined. Preserved artifacts filled the rooms to the ceiling for all to see the cruelties forced on nations of people. With mixed emotions we were able to put a human face to a very sad moment with an unexpected encounter of an elderly gentleman wandering through these rooms of torture. He'd suffered first- hand experience as a Jewish prisoner incarcerated in these buildings. Flanked by members of his family, his body language spoke a thousand words, as he showed us his tattoo of numbers. I know he was shocked when I spontaneously hugged him as he retreated back to his family.

Traveling has opened my eyes to the many wonders of this world. There are places to be and places to see. At first the motorcycle trips overseas were meant to experience the difference. Then I began to see sides of life that for many, was a struggle just to stay alive. I was asked more than once why I would consider visiting these places. At first I didn't understand why they would even wonder. I wanted to see the difference and why not?

Visiting the city of Berlin and 'Checkpoint Charlie', as the Wall was finally coming down we saw the freeing of people from an otherwise non-existent life as we Westerners know.

Krakow in the 'ghetto' told tales that could be fodder for horror movies. On the lighter side, we also enjoyed part of the Anniversary Celebration of the retrieval of land from the seas in Holland. All the places we rode to, although more than interesting, didn't compare with the horror of visiting two War Memorials, Dachau and Auschwitz Concentration Camps.

The first to visit was Dachau and as bad as it was, I couldn't imagine another being worse. There was…

Walking through the gates (with barbed wire and ghosts of armed guards in towers) I felt like I was walking on Holy Ground. This was a burial ground and the screams of a people are still calling out over the inhumanities forced on them in this camp. As a woman, saddest to me was the knowledge that these grounds had been used primarily for the experiment and extermination of women.

The rectangular, red brick, three story building we entered, gave you the feeling of any high school in America. Once inside though, you saw that the doors to the glassed-in rooms were locked. You could see the room's contents. Selected items were chosen for each room. One room was full of baby and small children's shoes tossed into piles. Another room was filled to capacity with crutches, canes and every type of leg and arm brace. Another was full of empty suitcases and bags that once held the last worldly possessions of the prisoners.

In the hallways there was no lack of photos. Passport-type mug shots of Mothers, Sisters and Daughters lined the walls. Dressed in drab black and gray stripes, their names, age and camp numbers were placed above their breasts. There were pictures of prisoners in various stages of torture. One I remember vividly was of a naked person (couldn't tell the gender) standing in a barrel of water, in a snowstorm waiting to freeze or die. Whichever came first.

I saw pictures of hospital equipment used in experiments on the young, the old, twins, the mentally retarded and the sick. Saddest of all was the photo of three little boys.

They were lying beside each other and appeared to be sleeping, but looking closer you could see a bullet hole between their eyes. Memories of that photo follow me today when I remember that day from Hell.

As my friend and I wandered throughout the building, we descended down a flight of shallow cement steps leading to the basement. At first we thought we were looking at empty fireplaces. We were wrong. The only heat that came from those bricked-in cubicles would have been from the prisoners, who had to stand with no food or water until they died.

Prisoners were forced to crawl into these airless, windowless oven-like miniature rooms and then forced to stand up. Each space would possibly hold four to eight people. They were then locked in and left for those in charge to monitor to see how long it took to suffocate that number of people. I didn't know my friend was slightly claustrophobic. Seeing her read the plaque that explained what she was looking at, I saw her bolt out of the room, gasping for air, while crying and screaming obscenities only she and I could hear. We fled the building together.

We escaped sights our minds couldn't comprehend. What kind of people would do this to another and why? For the two of us there would never be an answer that would satisfy us at that moment and probably never could. This camp was the worst. It left nothing to the imagination of evil and what better way to eliminate a race than attack the most vulnerable, Mother and her Child. These people endured atrocities we in our worst nightmare couldn't imagine. Even the metal sign over the entrance to one Camp, "ARBEIT MACHT FREI" which means **"work makes you free"** was one more cruelty to a doomed people.

As a Memorial to the victims of the Holocaust, the site of the camp surprises you with its' park-like appearance. Reminders of the past are preserved in the form of inscribed plaques of the number of dead or a hedged-in area where the ashes of thousands have been buried. The killing ovens are clean now. Flowers are placed at the entrance to the rooms. The gas chambers are sealed off. The walls and grounds scream of the pain these people suffered and my feelings were, 'I want out'! For me there was a choice.

'Dear Lord, Thank you for letting me live and laugh again, but please don't ever let me forget that I cried.'   Anonymous

Krakow Poland 1992

The gravestones stand silent in the stone walled-in yard beside the
synagogue in Krakow. No flowers are present but small stones are
placed on the Memorials as a tribute to the loved ones resting place.
This graveyard survived because of the churches tiny stature and went
unnoticed by the enemy during World War 2.

We entered the church quietly as the service continued. Standing at the
entrance an elderly woman offered Yamakas to the men. She hesitates
because I am next in line. I recognize her confusion and I say "No
Thank you." I know she was confused and she gave me an
embarrassed smile.

In describing my appearance, I am quite tall and that year I had a short
'mushroom-cut' hairstyle. I was also wearing blue jeans, which was not
the norm for older women in Poland. Once she heard my voice she
knew what not to do – I think.

Bernkastel– Kues Germany

The older man stood quietly watching as we parked the bikes. We changed from our riding leathers to casual walking shoes and a light weight jacket. He was of average build, in his later years and had a gentle look and smile. It was the smile that attracted me to say 'Hello' and encouraged him to come over. He carefully scrutinized the bikes and in a sweet Austrian accent asked us questions about our riding and where we came from. He might have recognized the rental sign over the UK plates so we may not have lived in England.

Interest in our being older women sometimes is the major source of conversation during these encounters.

We spoke for a few moments and just as we started to continue on, he gently said "you realize of course, we are not accustomed to *ladies of your age* riding motorcycles?" We smiled back and agreed "yes we knew."

I suppose we might have been a wee bit upset, but why? He only spoke of what we already knew. Those few words sometimes made our day. It's a pleasant reminder of perhaps a more gentle time but like everything else, it's good that some things have changed.

1994 Trier Germany

Maybe it was my clothes or maybe my height. But whatever it was I certainly drew the attention of an elderly woman seated in the Hotel's dining room that evening in Trier.

That day had been yet another wet and particularly testy ride. At that point, any Hotel would have been fine as long as we could get off the bikes and dry out. After a day of riding like that one I suppose we're allowed to be a bit feisty and it would be through no one's fault.

Luckily, Hotel Trier offered dry underground parking and wonderful rooms with all the amenities of a 4 star Hotel in America. Once we dried off and dressed in our best dry clothes, we ventured down to the dining room for a warm supper and then early to bed.

It was while we were waiting for our meal that my companion's attention was diverted to a female patron of our age, sitting across from us and staring.

Her attire was certainly different than ours. I remember she was wearing a wool A-line skirt with a toned-down plaid jacket and of course the sensible walking loafers seen on most women our age in Germany.

We had on our best sweat -shirts, blue jeans and western boots or runners (I don't remember which) and of course, our makeup and jewelry.

My friend seemed annoyed that the patron kept staring at me...*my back was to the patron so I wasn't aware of what was going on.* It upset my friend enough that she said to her I was "a woman." I had never thought of myself looking anything but and maybe that wasn't the problem…

After their momentary confrontation we finished our meal and retired to our rooms.

Next morning while loading our bikes at the main entrance, the same patron came through the glass turnstile and stopped. Now her look was different. Instead of the questioning looks she now understood what we were all about.

Women, leather, motorcycles… We smiled at each other and I said "Guten Morgen" and then we went about our own way. It was a much better way to end a relationship that had never gotten started but now, there was an understanding.…

Swiss Culture Clash 1996

Some European customs can be different than ours and the acceptance of nudity in various countries is more liberal compared to our practices in North America.

Nude statues, nude sunbathing and public use of pools in the nude can be quite common. For some of us it might be embarrassing.

We were traveling in Germany around the Bodensee and adjoining countries on our return trip. My friend was new to this area and suggested we find lodgings in Dachau. The time of year was off-season in September so some Hotel's were either closed or only renting part of the hotels' complex. Our lodgings that night included the full use of a pool, sauna and exercise room – supposedly for us alone- we thought.

The first thing we did once we had unloaded the bikes was headed for the pool with later plans for an early supper. We were changing from our bathing suits into dry clothes when we heard the sound of someone wearing flip-flops walking behind our cubicles. We were shocked to see a man wearing *just* flip-flops and a towel thrown over his shoulder in the change room. We quickly finished changing and went back to our room.

That evening was an early one and after a little chit-chat we settled in for the night. The next morning my friend decided to go for an early swim. She put on her bathing suit and was once again surprised to find this time the pool full of only men. She then realized she was the only one *with* a bathing suit on. She again retreated back to our room.

Later that evening as the dining room filled up, my friend seemed to shrink in her seat as she recognized the faces coming in. The same faces from the pool. Chances are they didn't even recognize her but that didn't lessen her discomfort. I think this is called a *culture shock,* to her anyways because it happened a few times on that trip.

The next day our journey led us into the Alps looking for a BMW Rally at the Abländschen Swiss Chalet, high up in the Swiss Alps. With previous knowledge forwarded to them by the bike rental that we would have no sleeping facilities, the Club graciously arranged sleeping accommodations for us. They were not quite what we might have expected.

After the trip to the Chalet and dealing with a bit of jet lag, we'd resigned early to bed and each of us chose an outside bunk. Our beds for the night were housed in a large dorm sized room with bunks lined up tightly beside each other, eight bunks wide. To get in your bunk you climbed up and over the end of the bed and crawled under the wool blankets. We were told that a family, husband, wife and child were going to be sleeping in the same room. We were comfortable with that knowledge and went to sleep.

The next morning we awoke to find all the bunks full of men and not a female in sight. The family had cancelled.

In the morning we walked into the only washroom to find the sinks lined with men in gauchies and sox and again not a woman in sight. Men with shaving crème on their faces, greeting us with a "Guten Morgen" was indeed different. We quickly headed for a stall and changed our clothes. After those few moments, breakfast was served and we certainly were made to feel very welcome.

Later we spoke to the members who expressed their pleasure that we had joined them having traveled all the way from America. I also spoke to riders who were great friends of another traveling companion, my friend from Florida who would have been with me on this trip but for a tragic accident in Mississippi riding to Show Low to meet me.

Some things are different now but some things are not. It is a small world.

Abländschen Switzerland 1996

Abländschen Switzerland was the site for the BMW Rally which was somewhere in the Swiss Alps. On this trip my companion and I had rented BMW's. The Bike rental agent asked us if we would like to attend the Rally. My companion was a member of a BMW Club in Ontario, so we both thought it would be an added pleasure to meet riders in a European Club.

We were different riders but the same. I'm a Gold Wing Rider and belonged to a Ladies Touring Club in America and was used to staying in Motels and Hotels. She was a BMW rider who toured and normally camped a good part of the time. We were compatible and the adventure of staying in a Chalet interested both of us.

We were given directions for our first day on the road. We followed the instructions faithfully but as the day wore on we began to wonder if we were anywhere close to the Rally. We did see a wooden sign eventually that was pointing up a steep gravel hill. Gingerly we followed it to find the entrance closed with a chain barrier.

Now we were on some biker's worst nightmare. Bikers hate hills and gravel. We were even hesitant to get off the bikes to turn around. The side stands on these bikes was another story waiting to be told. The only decision that made any sense was to make a **16 point** turn. We carefully turned the bikes around. Once we were heading back down, in our mirrors, we saw a car/driver patiently sitting, watching us. He *wasn't* there before! We were so in-tuned to turning the bikes around we failed to see the driver get out of his car, remove the barrier and then just sit and wait.

It must have been amusing for him but not a fun time for us. We later found out that we had come to the Abländschen service entrance. I would want to bet they didn't deliver their supplies by motorcycle.

Annecy and the Nun

One of my favourite cities in France stands on the shores of a crystal clear lake. Lake d' Annecy is

surrounded by rugged snow-tipped peaks. It was there that I witnessed an encounter between a Nun and a Mime that I will forever remember.

The rain came down gently as the sun continued to shine. Illuminating raindrops on roses that created a sparkling diamond effect along our path to the old walled-in city of Annecy. Our paved walkway between our Hotel and the city followed the edge of the lake. Leading through a topless bathing beach to the shoppes, one more example of the different customs we were not used to.

Here in this cobble-stoned old city, the canal bridges are festively decorated with continuously blooming flowers. The 12th Century Palais de l'Isle, once home to a Court of Law and prison, is now a small museum of local history. On the bridge overlooking the prison was the setting for a momentary encounter of a group of Nuns and a Mime.

I first saw the Mime standing rigidly alone on the aging bridge, a very good likeness of a Pope. He was then approached by a group of Nuns.

The Sisters stood looking and talking to/or about him for what we westerners might call a 'pregnant' moment and then wandered on chatting amongst each other. Moments later a single Nun came back and stood but then she pointed at him. I couldn't hear her words if there were any, but it looked as though she was chastising him for pretending to be someone, he was not. She then left.

This was a private moment I will never forget. Luckily I had my camera to document my moment in time with a series of shots with all subjects present.

Our journey to Annecy was one of many side trips taken that year-2000, the Millennium Year. My International Club held a celebration Rally in France. Members from all over the world were present. The grand meeting was held at Domaine de Seillac with various outings planned. We could then enjoy what this part of France had to offer. After the Convention, my companion and I headed to Annecy and then on to Italy. This trip would take us to some of the most famous cities in the World including Venice, Paris, Geneva, Dieppe and London UK.

My days in Annecy left me with memories I would like to repeat and know I never will. I have my photos though and it has been said "a picture can say a thousand words." Imagine the white swan and her three goslings beside the dock, farther out in the bay a lone black swan. The young girl with head phones (roller skating to music only she could hear) all beneath the black cloud over Lac d' Annecy. While the sun is peaking out below, casting sunshine on arbors of trees leaning over the canal, touring boats docked – waiting.

83

As we head out of town we HAD to visit the newest Harley Davidson Shoppe that just opened for business. This store was exceptionally big having a separate restaurant/café and a vintage vehicle motif. When traveling with a Harley rider, it is a must (for some) to visit with Mr. D. One more time a Honda rider was buying a T-shirt for another Harley rider. He is a special friend who I know would never ride here to visit 'MY' Annecy. I know he would appreciate a Harley shirt from France. One more glorious day to put in my bank of memories...

Up, Up, and Away 1998

Destination: Tintern Abbey, South Wales U.K.

The history of this Abbey was the same as many except that this one has stood proudly as a testament to the great skills of the medieval designers and craftsmen.

The building itself was founded for the Cistercian Monks in 1131 and was considered the wealthiest Abbey in Wales but would have begun to decay by 1536. As King Henry VIII appropriated the wealth of Religious Houses, so many became roofless as their lead was plundered. But there she was, she had withstood the hands of time.

After a long ride from the Port of Fishguard to Chepstow, we finally parked our bikes. Once unloaded, we changed from road grime leathers to walking clothes then wandered around the grounds of Tintern Abbey before dinner. Being familiar with the area my friend guided me along a lesser walked path over low two step fences and areas generally left for the cattle to graze. We walked quietly, as a solo swan drifted beside us in the slow moving waters of the Wye River - watching us. A family of Highland cows raised their heads, aware of our presence. The air was so still that not a leaf or twig rustled. We walked over a stone bridge and the area opened up as we rounded a hedge of bushes to a clearing large enough for a tailgate flea- market leaving enough room to inflate a hot air balloon.

Fascinated, I watched as the balloon was inflated. Its panels became larger and rounder and then I could read the name Bristol Rentals. Excited, I said, "I always wanted to go up in one of those!" "Then quickly, go and ask", my companion said. "But what if there's no room?" "You won't know unless you ask", she said patiently.

I did and moments later, I was climbing into the Gondola, retrieving my camera from my friend and slowly ascending into the sky.

This launch was a Sunset Champagne Flight and the balloon was NOT tethered. There were seven of us including the Pilot. The only sound I remembered was that of the burners lighting and heating the air in the balloon, as we were gently pulled up…up…

What my eyes now saw was so different. Skeletal Tintern Abbey was below me with the River Wye appearing as a slow writhing snake, winding itself around the Abbey. Looking down you could imagine a different life and times. The Abbey looked so much smaller now but you could identify some rooms and corridors with the facade of the building being the most prominent.

Looking down at the landscape, blocks of land resembled a board game. Sheep reminded me of hatpins on an imaginary cushion while the roads wound along the hedge as ribbons in cloth.

We floated as a feather in the breeze for about an hour as the sun began to set. The Pilot always had to be aware of the retrieval crew below us and as it grew dark he lost them. It reminded me of a serious cat and mouse game. Without the relay information of our position, they wouldn't know where we landed.

The crew had to know the directions and there was always concern that if we landed in the wrong field, the property owner could refuse entry to his land. Permission must be granted to enter his property.

Some farmers did not appreciate their chickens being frightened, especially when something was falling from the sky. (*The sky is falling!*)

All went well. The crew was able to find us and they were given proper permission to retrieve the gondola and passengers. It took very little time to load up the gondola on the trailer and all seven of us rode back to the Hotel in the van. The balloon had drifted about 1½ hours away from base, landing in an unknown area that evening.

What a feeling! If not for my friend mentioning Tintern Abbey and Wordsworth in her letter, my dream to ride in a hot air balloon might never have happened. I remember my words to her in a return letter. She spoke of places I could only dream of and her answer was, "I'll take you there someday." Words from Wordsworth described "the Landscape with the quiet of the sky." There was no sound except the hiss of the burners and the land was "as green to the very door."

With the quietness and beauty of that evening, the satisfaction of fulfilling my lifetime dream came true. In that hot air balloon ride, for those short sweet hours, in my world, "time suspended as the world drifted by."

Ballinter Ireland 1998

Monastery as defined in the dictionary means *'a place of residence occupied by a group of people (esp. monks) who have retired from the world under religious vows.'*

When my friend mentioned that during our trip she would be teaching in a Monastery, I envisioned a hidden away from the world, small, stone castle-like building. I was more than surprised that day as we rode up the winding path past huge aging Weeping Beech trees and grazing cattle.

Ballinter was a splendid Georgian mansion built in 1750, designed by Richard Castle for John Preston, grandfather of the first Lord Tara. Manicured estate grounds of the 'monastery' nestled along the Boyne River was now a Conference and Retreat Centre operated by the Sisters of Sion. The Sisters purchased the house in 1965 and had developed it as an Adult Education Centre. Today the elegant rooms accommodate retreats, study sessions and conferences.

Once we parked our bikes at the rear of the building we were welcomed into the Sisters' house by staff members (nuns retired to the Monastery to serve or rest) and then we were shown to our rooms.

The rooms were comfortable having the necessities including a single bed, shelves for some foods, books and personal items. These rooms quite often housed students from all parts of the world. They come to learn the life expectancies of a Nun or occasionally to learn the language of the country host.

Meals for my friend and I were to be served in the east wing of the staff's quarters and foreign students were housed on an upper floor. After breakfast the students were taught by my friend in the opposite wing.

The last day of the convention, a grand dinner was served in the teaching wing. My friend and I attended the festivities. The Sisters and I enjoyed 'happy hour' in the Ballinter reception entrance for an evening of entertainment. We talked, listened and/or danced to music performed by a local group of entertainers. They had also invited a young Irish girl to dance for us. Not all of the Nuns wore full habits and the number that did was minimal. This was a different time for me. These women had traveled from all over the world and were gathering for the last few hours before departing to their respective homes. It was a privilege for me to be included.

During the five days my friend was teaching at the Conference Centre, I would dress into my riding gear, walk past the students in the Halls and load up my bike in the back to go on my daily excursions of various local towns. The Sisters were cordial but there was always a questioning look wondering who I was. I never attended classes or ate with them but I was always present in the morning walking the same halls on my way to somewhere. I don't know if they saw me ride out the driveway but there were two parked bikes and one never moved. Near the end of her teaching my friend snuck out for a few sweet hours and we went for a short ride together. Oh those memories….

My morning travels took me to Tara (mentioned in 'Gone with the Wind') Trim ('Braveheart' was partly filmed at the Castle) and a bus trip to visit the megalithic tombs of Newgrange and Knowth. As much as I enjoyed the solo trips around Ballinter, it wasn't as much fun alone. Riding on the opposite side of the road did keep me more alert. I was never comfortable on roads in Ireland for that reason.

After the classes were over, my friend announced to her students who owned the second bike. This time she received warm smiles with nods of approval. It was not common knowledge that my friend rode a motorcycle. She had said the reception of her riding has not always been favorable by some church officials.

The following morning after a few photos, the Sisters gave us food gifts of dainty morsels of smoked salmon and finger sandwiches for our travels. My free time during the evening hours gave me the opportunity to do some hand embroidery. My gift to the Sisters for their kindness, pieces of Irish linen especially created for them. That last day instead of just a smile as I passed Sisters in the hall, an occasional sister greeted me and said "Good morning Sister." Now I could handle that!

Gas Leak in Norway

All it took was three mechanics, 3 c-clamps, a 3" to 4" piece of plastic hose and some gasket gunk to stop the gas leak. As much as I love riding, my motto has always been "I ride them – I don't fix them!" If or when my bike breaks down I'm at the mercies of mechanics or dealerships. Oslo Norway had some memories I would choose not to repeat.

Over the last twenty some years, when traveling in America I have ridden nothing but Wings. I found them to be low maintenance if cared for properly and almost worry free. Now on the other hand when in Europe I have rented different brand bikes. In 1994 I rented an older BMW and after my experience with a gas leak I vowed NEVER to rent an older bike again. If I would have been someone with a little mechanical knowledge, the leak might not have been so problematic I'm sure but with no knowledge, well…

I do not deal well with breakdowns as limited as they have been. Another side of me comes out that I don't like. When traveling with a 'Sister' I not only had to watch my tongue, *patience not being one of my finer virtues,* I had to deal with this added complication.

We first discovered the leak while checking our bikes that evening in the hotel's underground parking lot. There she sat, in her own pool of gas. We quickly moved the bike to a dry spot and then spoke to the Concierge in the hotel to help us locate the first mechanic.

The next morning we babied the bike to the *hole in the wall*, called a garage. After cooling our heels for an hour and don't ask how much, we were on our way…until the next stop.

Again we sought a mechanic because the leak was back again and as will usually happen this was a Saturday afternoon. How many dealers want to work on a Saturday? Not too many, that I'm aware of.

After a wee bit of begging, he agreed to replace a hose and once more we were on our way, headed west.

We traveled quite a bit the next day always with the fear of running out of gas. The BMW had no gauge to tell me how much gas I had. That night once again we stopped to refuel the bikes, found lodging for the night, shut off the gas and went to bed.

The next day was Sunday and our route was to take us into the mountains of Norway. Eventually we stopped for gas (it's raining of course) when a few riders rode in to gas up. I asked if they'd help me but they either couldn't or wouldn't. We then approached the store attendant and with her assistance we located another mechanic - on a Sunday. The mechanic was *of course off duty* and had to be summoned from home. For a change this young fellow knew what he was doing. Using gasket gunk he stopped the leak. With his expertise he'd allowed me a carefree ride for the rest of the trip.

When I rented the bike I was told, "if I broke it – I fixed it." Great if I would have known how to fix it and that was when the vow was made, never rent an older bike again.

Experiences I'd had on this trip taught me how to handle some emergencies. Like it? No - but I have learned. Once home my Visa bill arrived and those little items cost something like $350.00 US dollars. Once again, it made me appreciate my Wing back home. I am fortunate most of the time.

The Dolomites

The Dolomites are a range of mountains dividing the Eastern Alps in Northern Italy. These vertical massifs are set in a feathery green forest to be seen nowhere else in the world. They would be the most rugged mountain passes I would ever ride. Switchbacks with stupendous views is but one of the reasons thousands of riders flock to the Dolomites. The Passo del Stelvio and the Grossglockner to name two, are well known for the figure eight loops, one way tunnels allowing little room for maneuvering plus the 33 switchbacks on the east side of the mountain and 27 down the west.

In August, vacation month of Europe, every sport bike known to man could at any given time be seen racing up and down the hairpins and sweeps. This is a racers heaven or (for some) could be hell.

I had no doubt in my ability to ride these mountains that year and with new companions, I thought if we took our time there shouldn't be a problem. A few days into the trip though we all realized these mountains were a presence to be reckoned with. Counting the number of days, bikes (8/9 during the first seven days) and riders of our group experienced some sort of difficulty. Mine would eventually send me home.

This trip had been in the planning stage for over 1 ½ years. My companions included my friend from Israel, her niece from Alberta and my sister-in-law from Ontario plus several I.M.T.C. members based in England.

My personal challenge was to ride this world famous range in the Dolomites and I was excited!

A few days after arriving at our chosen Hotel and my second excursion into the mountains I started to experience changes in my bikes performance while riding. For some reason my BMW K100RT (named the 'Red One') wasn't responding properly. Shifting gears and braking became more difficult, suddenly it would jump into neutral. Events were taking off in their own direction and I was losing control.

Panic began to play a big part and now I was scared! Riding into the hairpins my speed became slower to the point I was almost stopped but then she let loose. Panicking, I pulled on the front brakes! That was my mistake. I was thrown off the road. This time I remember thinking I would go down the mountainside. I know I was pleading out loud "Please make this stop!" and in that split second it was over.

I remember a gentle voice and someone holding my hand while I was lifted into the ambulance- alone. I heard sounds of cars and bikes stopping. Curious caring people asked if they could help. I felt panic but had enough forethought to ask my friend to take my passport and credit cards.

I felt so alone but knew I wasn't. I also knew my companions would be riding their bikes to wherever I was being taken.

Then I remember the shrill of the ambulance screaming its wig-wag siren weaving its way down and out of the mountains through small villages to the hospital in Brixen Italy.

I don't know how long the trip lasted but someone repeatedly asked my name until the ambulance trip was over. Italian speaking voices asked questions I couldn't understand. It was a fuzzy time. I remember having x-rays taken and during that time my companions caught up with me in Brixen. I was no longer alone.

I'd landed on my right hip again. Having injured it before, the pain was more intense although this time I was fortunate nothing was broken. I had proper gear on. The armour in the jacket and pants cushioned my fall and it felt like landing on a mattress. (*I did something right buying these riding clothes*) Aside from my badly bruised hip and pulled muscles throughout my right side nothing was broken except parts of my bike. There was no reason now for me to stay on tour. Along with losing faith in my bike, I had lost faith in myself and would never ride her in these mountains again.

Hindsight is a wonderful thing and sometimes we'd like to blame someone or something but I knew it was my fault. I had pulled on the front brakes and now had to deal with it. This trip had twists and turns that changed my expectations to the point I wished I could turn back the hands of time. Perhaps the trip was ambitious but so were the

96

others. I had ridden in many mountain ranges before so what made this one different?

Perhaps it was the bike. She hadn't been ridden for 2/3 years and now it was start-up, learn all- over time, again. I know some things change but this much? I'll never really know.

After the hospital released me I was taken by taxi to the next Hotel on our Itinerary, Trafoi Italy. There I made the decision to return home to Canada. The 'Red One' was ridden away from the accident scene by a club member, back to our former Hotel's underground parking to have its future determined at a later date. I was told much later that the front brakes were mushy, the brake pads were worn down to bare metal and the clutch was adjusted three times to get her back to Corvara.

Leaving the group in Trafoi was a sad time. Club members assisted with plans for the placement of my bike then helped me arrange my travel plans to go home.

As a group we felt a loss of something that could have been so much more but was never meant to be.

The taxi ride to Munich was an endurance test and then a sleepless night in the airport. With no place to go until early morning, I carefully positioned my injured hip on an overnight bench in the Munich Airport and waited until dawn for the ticket booths to open. By 9pm most of the commuters were gone. Restaurants were closing as clean-up staff prepared for the next day.

It was quiet except for the floor polishing buffers as late employees hurriedly left the almost silent turnstiles. The airport was so big. Glass is everywhere with high angular walls to reflect the morning's light.

97

Who would have thought I'd be sleeping on a bench waiting for the booths to open and go home so soon, 11 days early and I was alone once more.

Anxious for the first rays of sunshine, the night was so long. When the booths finally opened I requested an aisle seat in the plane to avoid my hip being bumped.

It only took a few days to recover once I was home. Phone calls from those still on tour encouraged me to get back on my Wing. They knew that mentally I had left the trip wounded. Self-esteem is as easily broken as a bone and at that point, mine was fractured.

The encouragement of my husband and good friends, plus a few days of rest, I finally got 'back in the saddle' and my life was back to almost normal.

I'm more cautious now, but hopefully more observant. I WILL have more days on the road. *I just have to remember those blasted front brakes...*

Foods to remember...or not

Traveling in the many countries over the years certainly has been interesting and pleasurable. However, I was usually accompanied by an old enemy- pancreatitis. It usually didn't stop me from traveling but I had to know where the closest hospital was to my Hotel – whatever country I was in. I never knew which foods triggered the attacks. Foods highlighting various times making the trip more memorable included...

Bergen Norway – wonderful Ox meat dish with dark cream gravy served in a candle-lit ambience. The candles, the miniature lights and the service - never to be forgotten...

Poland – raspberry banana sundae with no ice cream... I have to learn Polish to get the ice cream I guess.

Abländschen Switzerland – meatless dinner served under a tent with cold pickled veggies and a block of Swiss/type cheese melted under a gas burner and served on hard bread. I still haven't found that type of burner or cheese in America.

Esher England – The smell of smoked Herring served at breakfast early in the morning still nauseates me.

Chester England – Fish and Chips with mashed peas... They would never convince me that large peas taste good – mashed...

Wisconsin Dells, Wisconsin – Imitation lobster, my stomach didn't like that one and I ended up in emergency with a Pancreatic attack. Old problem, different food...

99

Sheridan Wyoming – Dairy Cream with hot chocolate sauce and fresh raspberries. New treat to me and to die for

Yakima Washington – Scallops shared with my companion, the absolute elite in Seafood.

Bernkastel – Kues, Germany…a favourite city in Europe and sugar-free Apple Strudel. Need I say more?

Clausthal-Zellerfeld Germany – OJ and wine. After a long dark ride up the mountain we begged the Gastoff owner for something to drink. Ending a long memorable day we would choose not to repeat. It seems no one serves food after 1am…

Near München Germany – '*horsey- dervies*' creativity at its finest

Heidelberg Germany – Bratwurst on a bun (*no sauerkraut*) sold by a street vendor. Is there any other way?

Germany (on the road) "Special of the Day" – Spaetzle and smoked ham. I have a dislike for anything smoked and the disapproving look the waitress showed was quite noticeable after I set aside every single morsel of cubed *smoked* ham…

New York State – refried beans in a Mexican Restaurant reminded me of warm-ups at home. Yuk!

Lake George, NY – Steamed white fish and fresh green beans prepared in an upscale restaurant. Stomach acting up again and it still tasted 'dead.'

100

Navan Ireland – *Smoked* salmon, a thoughtful gift from the 'Sisters.' I gave my share to my companion…

Riquewihr France – An aperitif before dinner set up my perfect lamb stew dinner and fresh broccoli for disaster. Wine and my stomach – non-compatible…

The memories of some of the meals added colour to the difference I always looked for. In my memories one scene plays back quite often. It was the first time we stopped at a sidewalk café in France. We parked our bikes to relax after a long days ride. I savored my very first Cappuccino as we watched the world pass by. My thought at the time; "I wonder what the poor people are doing?"

Miscellaneous Stories

In the face of Mother Nature

Riding can be a test to ones abilities and determination. The desire to continue, knowing the circumstances will eventually change is the fuel most riders own. Trips are often remembered by the temps at their extreme and must be dealt with. When embarking on a road trip, there are no guarantees.

Most of us do not have the luxury of waiting to continue on. We go on being left with the memories Mother Nature has given us. There are times she can be our 'best friend' or our 'worst enemy.' How we manage to survive the weather's diversity is the challenge to all our abilities. So there will be times we will smile just remembering…

1992 - St. Quentin Fr. A dark RAINY morning in France heading out on the Autobahn wearing a yellow bib-overall and jacket, *construction* rain suit. I'd altered the style but forgot about the wind factor at speeds of 60 – 70 miles per hour. The forgotten wind blew me up like the Michelin man or even more like Big Bird. We quickly pulled off the highway, my companion and I exchanged my bungee net for her cords. We tied the cords around my waist and the problem was solved. Next time I would have to remember to snap the pockets down. They'd made a perfect well of water for *fish* but the rest of me stayed dry. Smiles from construction workers working on the side of the road that day were certainly curious.

1996 — Würth Germany. The memory of terrible Fog and Rain while we followed the tail lights of a tour bus up a *dark* mountain still brings back a fear of veering off some mountain roads.

That early evening we also had another problem. My troublesome headlight at times was as bright as the light of a candle. When I unknowingly turned it off, my companion panicked. In the heavy fog she could no longer see me behind her and quickly pulled over to the side of the narrow road.

After we fiddled with the light we we're soon on our way again only this time without the buses lights to follow.

Thank God for friends and our traveling Angels. Together we rode into a small mountain village, a sanctuary for skiers and motorcycle riders. A brightly lit Chalet offered everything a soggy rider could want. Warm, dry bedrooms — *available,* a cozy dining room with home cooked smells coming through the kitchen door and a warming good night's rest made us feel human again.

The next morning we awoke to streams of brilliant sunlight peeking through our lace curtains. We heard Swiss Brown cow's bells as they were being herded up our road back into the hills. A visit to a Honda dealer later that day solved the problem of the 'candle' light.

1996 The Black Forest in Germany is a range of mountains. Deeply forested, and known for its beauty along with spa facilities, Alpine skiing, castles and magnificent fir forests.

Although beautiful to the eye, *RAIN* is as wet in Germany as it is in Canada. When you get dumped on, the only thing you can hope for, is a place to get out of its' way.

That day a bus stop did quite well. Luckily the downpour stopped, the sun came out and we were able to join in the festivities at a local village fair. We parked in the parking lots' only patch of sunlight. Spreading our riding gear over the windshield and seat with our gloves perched on the rear view mirrors, I remember with a smile… She made me think of her as my 2 wheeled buddy who gave me comfort on my travels, shared my adventures and even served as a traveling clothesline.

2000 St. Bernard Pass, Italy with waist high *SNOW*, wet paved roadways and rivers of melt water flowing across our paths around the hairpin turns on our way to Venice.

Winter months in Canada are not my favourite time of year and I thought, 'if I wanted snow all I had to do was stay home.' In a few months I could have all the snow balls I wanted. Fun in the snow this time was seeing my companion make a stand-up snow angel against the snow bank and then throwing a snowball at me.

Awesome mountain views, brilliant sun bouncing off the snow caps and it wasn't even cold! It was perfect because this time I could ride even with the snow.

2001 Peterborough Ontario Canada brings back memories of the 'Ghost' being blown over after stopping at the end of a driveway to check our maps. The strong *WIND* was so persistent. It created sand swirls on the 401 and 407 highways that Mothers Day.

This was the first long distance ride of the year and I was pumped. When the 'Ghost' went over, with a little help from the wind, we quickly picked her up and continued on. We had friends waiting…

2003 Tornado Alley in Minnesota was a mystery to the six of us until we watched the news that evening. 50+ touchdowns and we weren't aware of anything except the on and off of the *WIND, SUN AND RAIN*. Mother Nature was at her best of the worst.

The interesting part during that whole day was the number of clothes we changed during the different weather changes. At one point we had everything on including jackets, chaps and gloves. A few hours later it was so hot we couldn't take enough clothing off. Changing again, but this time into rain suits and feeling like we were in a sauna. All this changing made possible because of the storage in one more piece of equipment trailing at the back of the bikes- that wonderful Bushtec trailer.

Couldn't believe you could get six women's wardrobes in one trailer. These are truly the days of modern day miracles.

2005 New Brunswick Construction roads in the *RAIN* and especially slippery clay might cause a bike and trailer to go down. At that point I was taking my time but unknown to me the lead was wondering what happened as I disappeared out of sight. A construction pickup somehow got in between me and my friend. It didn't help any when a worker walking along beside her could hear her 'oh shit', 'oh shit', 'oh shit' as she struggled to control her bike. There was no reason to worry but at that moment neither of us knew different a-n-d we didn't dump the bikes. We rode out of the construction and caught up to each other, nothing was wrong and we just continued on.

2005 Temps of 100/110 F, in South Dakota created waves of *HEAT* that rippled and shimmered ahead of us on the Interstate to Sturgis. After dinner that evening, for a short glorious hour, riding our bikes and listening to music, we rode double-up out of town. We were racing up and down the rolling hills into the setting sun with the temps changing in the hollows of the road. The ride didn't last long in the cool but was enough to be appreciated.

Some might say they wouldn't travel in weather that is less than perfect. But if they take that inconvenience seriously they could miss out on an otherwise good trip.

Proper gear, a dependable bike, a compatible traveling companion but mostly the riders who willingly continue is the quality needed to do this type of traveling.

It is said to try and explain to a non-rider would be futile. I only know that for me when I remember those times, I can smile and wish they would be repeated.

To ride is to live, to live and to love. That's what it's all about, the love of riding. Give me back the last years and I'd gladly do it all again.

Even in the face of Mother Nature.

Down the Rabbit Hole…2004

As a biker I have had experiences that have coloured my whole being. I have laughed, I have cried and I have learned.

My riding started at the mature age of 43 and for the past 20 years my journeys have taken me to all parts of the North American Continent, as far north in Europe as Norway, east to Northern Italy, south to France and west throughout England.

In 2004 my travels took me to the Italian Dolomite Mountains and it was while I was navigating the world famous hairpin turns I went down - twice.

I was left physically and emotionally shaken. As I gradually began to heal, I knew eventually the Dragon and I would meet again. I knew of only one way to succeed and I'd want to be alone on roads comparable to those in Italy.

Once I was back in Canada, weeks after the European trip, I chose to ride the only curves I knew that were similar (certainly not as many) down the Niagara Escarpment in the Stoney Creek/Grimsby Ontario area. This is my story…

The road was there, I just had to go down it and when I did, the Demons were waiting.

The mind is a devious creature at times and can selectively choose to forget important details that might count. Details like how many hairpins there were and better still the 'rabbit hole.' I might have backed off that day and let the events take place another time but this was not to be. Once committed to riding down the mountain there was no turning back.

107

The Road was steeper than I remembered and seemed so much more now. The turns weren't as wide as I would want them but this time there weren't as many, I just had to get through these few and maybe…

The first curve widened and then suddenly, turning inward it became gradual and then disappeared around the side of the mountain, reminding me of a rabbit hole. In its 'den' the road straightens out for a fleeting second. I can't see the oncoming traffic and if I went too wide maybe…my hearts pounding. I can feel it! My arms are shaking, but that curve is over! "Let the bike do what it can, she's not the 'Red One' *(BMW)"* I kept telling myself.

"Let the 'Ghost' work, *(white wing)* let her find her way around. There now, just a few more and were done."

The next bend was gentler but I can see the traffic behind crowding us. "Get back, leave us alone!" I wanted to scream.

"Slow down, take it easy."

The road is changing. "It's straightening. It's over!" Those were words only I could hear but I could feel them.

That day was the test. It had to be. Events in the near past brought fears I didn't think were possible and to 'get back in the saddle' I had to 'bite the tail of the Dragon.' This time he didn't bite back.

I had done it. I know this fear might be a demon ever present but will be only as difficult to overcome as I will allow it. Another day… Probably, but not with as much fear and the ever-so-fragile self-esteem can live again.

In a heartbeat 2005

His smile was nice, almost familiar and a welcome change on that fifth day while riding in the rain and pulling a trailer sentimentally named 'the Pup.' This was her second inaugural ride with testy wet weather nipping at the edge of my nerves.

My thoughts during those days were, "if I could get rid of her and ship her back home, she'd be gone in a heartbeat." At that moment though in the truck stop, all my concerns were put on the back burner while my friend and I enjoyed a conversation with this complete stranger who would later be described as my 'road angel.'

We grew increasingly testy as we drew closer to that day's goal. The main obstacle for my companion was keeping warm and dry. She had unknowingly left her warm clothes at home and she was cold. The only comfort for us was the knowledge that our MM friend was waiting for our arrival giving us energy to continue, on this unpleasant day.

I know my thoughts concerning the trailer were strictly between my ears. Inner doubts made me wonder if I was going too fast, too slow, and how was 'she' reacting in the curves or on the wet roads. With all the what-ifs that could be imagined. The 'pup' was doing nothing wrong! I knew the two accidents in Europe were bringing back those shades of the past and adding colour to my insecurity. I had fought these demons and thought I had won the war but they were rearing their ugly heads again.

Our 'road angel' was a truck driver but he also rode a Harley in New Brunswick. We biker talked for an hour and it was a welcome relief on

109

this not so pleasant day. The subject eventually turned to my trailer and the what-ifs. Out of the blue he offered to take my trailer home for me.

He was working out of New Brunswick and would be traveling to Ontario. It was interesting that I trusted him up front but could I follow through with the plan?

I know I said I would have shipped the trailer back but would I or could I? What would be Frank's response when I told him what I was planning? It was a Christmas gift. He had worked on it for so many weeks and was so proud to see me pull it.

I called him and explained why I didn't want to pull her any longer. He, of course had questions as to how I would handle this predicament. Being the supportive husband he was, he agreed with whatever arrangements I could make. At this point, my well- being on the road was imperative.

My decision included meeting the trucker and his wife a few days later on the Trans Canada Highway near Gagetown New Brunswick. They were headed to St. Catharines Ontario (my back door) for a week's vacation. So everything seemed in place. Until… coupling the 'Pup' to his van, we found the hitches were not compatible and alternative plans were necessary.

At that point we were staying at our friend's home in Gagetown NB. After the new arrangements were put together I chained the trailer temporarily to a telephone pole in their yard. The new plans were with the owner of the Transport Company in Wolfville Nova Scotia.

During our wait for new directions, our Nova Scotian MM friend, another MM from Maple Ontario, plus my companion and I toured

110

the Gagetown area. She led us on back roads, bridges and 10-minute ferries to areas we would never have seen otherwise. Now without the trailer I was free again!

Two days later, three of us headed for Miramichi NB, P.E.I, The Cabot Trail, Nova Scotia and then back into the States for our 65th Convention in Hagerstown Maryland.

Our three-day convention in Hagerstown was a good one with the renewing of old friendships, making new ones and the usual convention formalities.

This year was an election year and a Convention I will never forget. I was elected as Vice President. I had belonged to the Motor Maids for 24 years and never did I dream I'd one day be the Vice President. What an honor and to know I had so many friends with faith in my abilities was so encouraging.

One more week and I finally arrived home. After almost four weeks on the road I received an email from my friend in Gagetown that said 'as she wrote' my trailer was being loaded on to a flat bed trailer. She was on her way to Wolfville, NS. The 'Pup' was taking on a life of her own.

Another day and a phone call to inform me that I had left the wrong key to open the trailer. Go figure…

More plans now. Wait for a payload close enough for me to give the correct key to the driver.

The company owner is talking about renting or buying the 'Pup.' He wanted to use it to go to the Sturgis, SD Rally. Selling the trailer was not an option my husband would consider so now the 'rental' might be headed to the United States. The truck owner's reason for renting the trailer was to haul his wife's makeup. Huh?? I gently suggested he be kind.

Humorous to me was the 'Pup', the owner and myself might all be in Sturgis on the same dates. I had visions of a semi passing me on the Interstate, loaded with a Harley Davidson and a small white trailer looking all too familiar. I think the Angels had a twinkle in their eyes as they watched the picture unfolding.

It happens like that sometimes. I'm sure they have a sense of humour too. After all, with the nonsense going on around this trailer what else might they do? Just watch for what you wish for…

Americade 2006... The Dragon again...

I didn't know we would meet again until I started on a downward plunge of newly paved asphalt leading to our rented cottage in Bolton's Landing, NY and the 2005 Americade Rally.

He was nibbling at my heels again as I cautiously rode the path that was turning into curvy switchbacks downhill and feeling too familiar to be comfortable... My imagination was going places it shouldn't be. The 'Ghost' and I carefully rode down to an opening of nicely maintained cottages, manicured lawns and a private marina full of renter's boats. *We found out later it would take ½ hour of fast walking to get up that same hill.*

Well we made it but not without a lot of anxiety and I was not going to ride back up! Not me!

The Dragon didn't get me this time! Irrational thinking, I know, but my emotions were very raw on this trip. The sudden death of my son two weeks earlier would send me into an emotional tailspin that would leave me teary eyed and just plain shaky. So the Dragon's presence wasn't wanted – again...

The stubborn part of me came out and I announced to him and my world, "we are not going back up together!"

My Angels are always around me. They come in different forms, like the time I wanted to ship my trailer home while traveling through the Eastern Provinces and there he was.

113

This time after watching my *performance,* a cabin renter (Harley rider) pulling a trailer for his wife's wheel chair, came forward and offered to take the 'Ghost' back up the hill the next morning if I would load her up on the trailer.

A Harley motorcycle cop said he would ride her up the hill and yet still another, the Motel/Cabin owner, offered to take me up and down the hill in his golf cart whenever I needed. Although I was so very thankful for all of the offers, it didn't lessen the feeling of anxiety just knowing somehow 'we' had to get back up and how many times would this help be needed during our stay?

The decision eventually was taken out of my hands when one of my traveling companions (Gold Wing rider) rode the 'Ghost' back up the hill and our belongings were moved to a cottage closer to the top of the hill.

Whew! The Dragons tail didn't get stepped on and he didn't bite. Eventually this nonsense would have to stop.

The planned trip to Americade this year was the same as others but this time the weather was more than unsettled with a forecast of a cold wet front approaching in the next day or so. Riding the off-interstate roads to the Rally was very pleasant although one male member not used to anything other than the Interstates did a lot of grumbling about the many stops. We had planned the trip that way and for him, too bad, so sad. He did have an option and could leave anytime he chose or just adjust. He didn't leave so it couldn't have been that bad!

Darker clouds filled the sky the next day and our hopes that the unsettled weather would pass over, were gone. We'd paid our admission to various outings and looked forward to the next couple of

114

days. My friend had a problem with the CB on her almost-new bike and thought she might get some answers from BMW reps in the Vendors section of the Show.

A good portion of the day was wasted because she really didn't get any useful information. She also had a hard fall from her bike, badly bruising her kneecap thus adding more stress to possible activities.

Thinking her knee/leg would be better the next day (it wasn't) we woke up to almost torrential rain and decided it would be best to head home. The nasty weather was now pushing its way into Lake George, NY.

One might wonder sometimes, how's it possible to be heading west and then all of a sudden the signs are saying east? Well it happens. We rode three different routes through Syracuse, NY and all of them were headed a different direction. We really don't know how we did it and major construction in Syracuse didn't help. We were finally headed west again and trying to get onto I-90 west. We ended up going south on another 90 and again in cold rain. That day we couldn't do anything right and eventually we had to get a room for the night. At that point it didn't seem we would ever get home.

Americade that year didn't turn out like we hoped it would. Most times I can come away with something to smile about but this time it would be a real stretch of the imagination. Looking at the map the next day and seeing that we had ridden almost half the length of one of the Finger Lakes before we turned around might on a very good day, make you smile. Probably not!

115

Cameo

My preference for riding has always been the mountains. When I think of Kitzbuhel, Hallstatt, St. Johann, and Innsbruck Austria, these areas give a new meaning to what heaven must be about. On these roads and passes, I know exactly what my ride and I can do. We must be in synch to appreciate it. Nothing compares with feeling so capable because our destiny in is our hands.

That day was bright with a few light clouds and a brisk wind as we traveled along a road that wound itself through the Swiss Alps. This area during the winter is world renowned for winter skiing. The linking of 62 lifts creates a series of runs allowing a skier to travel downhill for more than 50 miles. We were enjoying the summer version of what the Alps had to offer. Traffic was almost sparse at times as we road beside a fast flowing river winding around the rocks in the gorge beside us. Ahead of us, hidden curves to test our riding skills thus allowing us a freedom we're always seeking. At one point the traffic began to back up, slowing our pace to a fraction of our speed. Soon traffic was turning around and coming back towards us.

We continued on until we saw what the disruption was. Highway crews were repairing a train track that would cross our route and they were rerouting the oncoming traffic. We pulled off the road to discuss our next move when we saw a worker pointing to us and waving for us to come forward.

As we approached him, he continued to wave us on and over the construction. There was no room for cars but we were lucky, we could continue on. *I have to mention that the repair, crossed over the river, and the river was many meters below the road's surface.*

116

We quickly looked at each other and without hesitation thought, "if they say we can go over, we can go over" but getting closer to the crossing, we saw what we had to travel on.

The highway worker had found a wide plank that straddled the river and he waved us over. For a brief mini-second, I thought "this is nuts" but it happened so fast, we rode on it and were again on our way.

I wish the workers could have seen the looks on our faces. If we would have had more time to think, we might have changed our minds. They seemed to know we could do it and we had no choice. Our looks could have been a Kodak moment.

Custer State Park, South Dakota 2003

I had been told that if I wanted to see Buffalo, I could see a *million* but I had to travel to Custer State Park USA. All the stories of the variety of animals I would soon see would be proof. While traveling on the Wild Life Highway I saw burros of every colour and pattern wandering on or along the road begging for a treat by those willing to stop. It was not unusual to see a burro poke its head into a car window or stand long enough for a picture.

The Wild Life Loop is 18 miles long and it passes through grasslands and rolling hills. It is home to many species of wildlife, including the stately Elk, Coyotes, Bighorn Sheep and Buffalo, mighty but also the most unpredictable.

We always tried to be aware of where they were and not disturb them.

One story that told of their unpredictability earlier that season was of a rider and his noisy bike startling a Bull that provoked an attack. When all was said and done the rider was taken to a hospital with severe injuries to his groin and his bike, a complete write-off. He was one of the lucky ones. He lived to tell the tale.

Women and the Necessities of Survival

When the rain and wind caught up with us that day we were booting down the highway in Ohio heading for Columbus. I felt 'it' crawling up my leg.

Panic took over and imagining the worst case scenario, I had to pull over but the traffic was such that I had to wait until it cleared up around me. In those critical moments I vainly tried to squash whatever it was with my free hand but the critter kept crawling towards some very private parts.

As soon as possible we all pulled over to the shoulder of the highway. I couldn't get off my bike fast enough. I urged one girl to help me pull my high cut western boot off while I undid my zipper and yanked my pants down.

To my relief it was just a flustered black horse fly that was probably trying to find a dry place too. Once free, believe it or not, he shook himself loose and flew away.

My imagination during those moments was certainly more creative then thinking it was just a fly. It *could* have been a snake....well it could have been!

All this action took only split seconds along that busy Interstate in a torrential downpour. I'm sure there weren't too many drivers passing us who were aware of what was happening on the side of the road. They didn't know sanity flew over my wet shoulder, the moment my safety and vanity was threatened.

119

Long Johns in Yellowstone

It was starting to get hot by afternoon and with the number of layers we needed that early morning, now was the time to take off one of them.

Of course there were no restaurants available so a wee bit of privacy could be found beside a girls own bike and why not? Would she have minded that picture of her taking off her pink long-johns that day?

One car going by thought the scene was interesting enough to honk his horn. Someone in our group of six, unknown to some of us, did take a picture. The next time the long -johns were seen was on a Convention Bulletin Board and it wasn't me- I promise. Some people can be so mean! LOL

Now I know…

Sometimes conversations between women are more than funny but also not really meant to be overheard by others. There are questions that really have no answers until 'it' happens.

While riding in cold rain with all the clothes needed to stay dry, you might wonder what it would feel like if you were caught short before you could make it to a public washroom. That day in Germany, she found out…

WARM!!!!…

A Girl's Gotta Do

Eastern Europe did not have the many luxuries we Canadians were accustomed to such as Laundromats around every other corner. To save on clothing wash time we would take with us female articles that might work to our advantage including disposable panty-liners.

It always pays to be prepared but this time we were caught in cold rain and everything we owned got wet including our only brand new box of panty-liners.

The solution of the day… Pray for a warm heated room and then dry them. Once we unloaded the bikes and retired to our room we did eventually place each and every liner on any flat surface available including lampshades and windowsills. Then, 'we did not open the door to any male person that evening."

That night could have been an embarrassment to both of us but necessary. A girl's gotta do, what a girl's gotta do…most of the time…

Lycra Lady

Some riders will wear their safety riding gear in all weather, even when the temps are in the high 80's and 90's. When the bike stops, off come the leathers and the rider might be wearing something light underneath for comfort.

Lycra shorts seem to be a favourite for some girls. They take little space and this is good – I suppose. The only disadvantage that I can see is that the general public doesn't usually see them and when they do, they could look like underwear.

That day we were traveling through P.E. I. in ungodly hot weather. Some of us wanted to see Ann of Green Gables homestead. Two others having seen it before decided to travel on to the next town to wait for us.

This was fine for all of us so when we were finished playing tourist my friend and I continued on to meet our group.

As we approached our meeting spot the 'Lycra Lady' must have thought we would miss each other. Pulling at her leathers, half on and half off, she ran out towards the road madly waving to us.

I'm sure the car driver who was honking his horn playfully that day, thought "one more, loose nut."

The Deere

All of us have interests at home that might attract us to the same while on the road.

Riders will look for Harley, BMW and Honda shoppes everywhere they travel and sometimes plan trips especially for that reason.

Truck stops are also popular and are known to offer good food at decent prices most of the time. They usually have a souvenir store as well as nice western clothes.

Tim Horton's coffee house chain has certainly drawn a lot of riders to their shoppes. Offering good coffee and light lunches, they are definitely one of my favourite stops.

A widely recognized name in my household too is John Deere and of course anything related.

My husband is a hobby farmer with over 100 acres to farm. He collects, restores and works on pre-60's era, John Deere equipment. Of course while I'm on the road I keep my eyes peeled for something I can take home. It could include old/new books, photos, collectable J.D. signs and perhaps some family history from friends who know of his interest.

With all this in mind, one day the subject amongst one friend and I was the yellow John Deere emblem.

It is known by J.D. enthusiasts that if the deer has four legs on the sign, the era is pre 1960. If it has two legs, of course it is newer.

Somehow during that trip one girl seemed to fixate on anything with a deer on it including highway signs, bulletin boards, farm equipment, anything.

I'm sure after that trip she never looked at any of those highway signs quite the same way again. Come to think of it, I wonder how many legs the highway deer sign does have? I can't say I've ever really paid attention to that *important* detail…hmmm…

Friday 13th – what's it all about?

I know I'm dating myself when I admit to knowing what it was like in the beginning. 25 years ago, in fact. It's interesting that Port Dover was then just a small dot on the Ontario road map. This quaint village (pop. under 1100) located where Highway #6 meets Lake Erie, did take claim to being the world's largest fresh water port though. You could also enjoy one of Arbors' famous foot long hotdogs along a beautifully clean beach. Then one day in the mid 80's Port Dover's status changed dramatically because of a small group of riders who wanted a different destination for their Friday the 13th ride.

From its early beginnings, Port Dover's reputation has grown from six or seven riders to over fifty thousand riders and still growing, that converge on this now famous town in Ontario.

For the uninformed one might wonder what reason brings so many riders to this busy little town now on the map. For a good number, the reason is simple *it's Friday the 13th* and why not? For some of us, it's a welcome habit. There are those who come for the shopping (if they can get close to the shoppes) but for most of us, it's the 24 hour parade of every type of bike seen on the road.

Clubs of same name brands, groups on sport bikes, touring riders with all the bells and whistles and even vintage bikes once more restored to their original glory. Trikes, homemade bikes, bikes with sidecars and bikes with trailers, you'll see it all. So if anyone asks, "Why go to Port

125

Dover?" I ask, "why not?" Where else will you see such a group of motorcycle riders of this stature during a blustering snowy day on December 13th *(you might be lucky and see Santa riding a bike)*. April 13th, so wet you squish when you walk and August 13th with all the heat you would want and need.

Gone are the days when you could arrive before noon, park your bike on the Main Street at any given time to sit and watch the other bikes roll in. Those were the days when shopping was a joy and the number of vendors was limited to but a few.

Now, finding a parking spot in the center of town, you have to be present before 9am and even then it's not a given. Streets are closed to through-traffic at both ends of town around 9:00am. Traffic is rerouted to side roads. The trick is to find a parking spot after the blockade is in effect. Clusters of Police block off Port Dover's entrances down to a single lane. During these times, certain bikers are pulled over and questioned about who they are, what they ride, and why they want to enter Port Dover. The reason is simple but necessary. The majority of riders are relatively harmless but because of some riders, the times are changing.

Remember the 1%er's? They are the riders who are not there for the riding. They have their own agenda, drugs, booze, stolen goods, etc. At the best of times, they are monitored by the police and tolerated by those who are not interested in their business.

Port Dover is different now but it's not. There are more people, more bikes and more cops but the original reason for the Friday the 13th gathering has not changed. It's a ride and what more need be said? Will I be riding to Port Dover October 13th? In a heartbeat! I hope to see a number of our Motor Maid white vests there too. It is true that history is sometimes created for just the wants of a few.

126

Comrades

Anecdotes

The last twenty-some years have been a learning time. I not only saw new parts of the world, I also developed lasting friendships. Each trip might be with a different traveling companion but at the end of the vacation, the friendships remained.

When I think back to the many good memories, most of the time I can put a name to the person I was traveling with. Some of the incidents might have been with a hint of laughter or some with a touch of aggravation but nothing destroyed the friendships. All we wanted to do was ride and we were the lucky ones, we did it together.

We discovered many differences that foreign countries had to offer as well as having to deal with what was thrown at us.

Nancy…at the time my companion from Florida, having many allergies, discovered wine manufactured in the Mosel River Valley in Germany had no additives. She was ecstatic! A hilarious time then was watching her coming out of a Gastoff in Bernkastel-Kues arms laden with bottles of wine. I don't remember how many, but we had to find space in *our* bikes to carry them the rest of the trip.

Muriel…Again in Germany this girl was creative and put together a banquet of foods to nibble on during a rainstorm. All the 'nibbles' were food stuffs that she and her companions had in their bikes. I can still picture her walking into our room with a paper plate above her

127

shoulder and a napkin on her arm announcing "horsey dervies" were now being served. Amazing what girls will eat when traveling.

Ruth…I don't know how they did it but this girl and her husband got so lost. They ended up in Czechoslovakia instead of Germany. At the end of the day they decided that any Gastoff would do. They finally stopped at the first one they could find. They entered the lobby and turned to see all of us sitting having dinner and wondering where they were. Our bikes were parked at the back of the building so they didn't see them. I'll never forget the look on their faces when they turned and saw us. Don't know how they got that turned around. That's really lost!

Connie…When the leader suffers from night blindness and the tail rider has the maps, night blindness and being lost can be synonymous.

Maureena…Famous for her ten minute(er), this Lady could close her eyes anywhere, anytime, and turn the world off for ten minutes then awaken, refreshed. Rules of the day… If she turned off and landed in her soup, I'd get up and say I didn't know her. It never happened.

Adriana.,,One phrase I'll never forget came from someone frustrated riding in the rain in the UK. She made the statement "this is not supposed to be a quest." It was funny to me but not for her.

Arlene…As well as you think you might know someone, there are times you really don't. Unknown to me in the beginning, this friend hated all bridges. In the lead most of the time when approaching one I would call it 'land over water' and she dealt with them. Gondola rides up mountains weren't a favourite either but being my friend she tolerated a lot. Once she was at the top of the mountain though she didn't move out of the restaurant until she had to. I didn't know she was claustrophobic too. That is a real friend.

128

Joan…I haven't seen too many girls put on PJ's to ride in the cold but this Lady did. It took a lot of years before she finally put all the right pieces of clothing *and bike* together to finally get warm in the cooler weather. Now when we have to ride in the cold weather (my preference) she enjoys the ride without the aggravation. She is at all times, a pleasure to travel with.

Audrey…This 'special' lady taught me all the good stuff about riding. Warts I learned on my own. One important rule was that 'you never turn around" for almost any reason. There were a few times we sat on the side of the road and waited and hoped that the lost were behind us. Quite often I saw the 'Cheshire cat smile.' Lost again…

Heidi…Call it vanity or forgetfulness some riders refuse to have glasses on while traveling. As long as you're following the leader sometimes it doesn't matter – to some. I could never quite understand how some manage to get there. I guess the name of the game is 'don't lose the leader.' Lord, help you, if you do.

Happy Birthday Maureena

Thinking about my friend Sr. Maureena brings back so many good memories it would be difficult to find one that would be more significant.

Many years ago both of us were relatively new to the club. I would never have dreamed that a few years later we would be companions on motorcycle trips that would take us to Europe.

I recall our first time together standing beside each other at the Sturgis, SD Convention picture not really knowing each other. Maureena then, was somewhat of an icon to me. Her lifestyle *and* the fact that she carried her computer behind her wherever she rode, interested me. Then, the Computer world was an unknown to me. I thought 'how unique she was.'

Good luck and the desire to travel in more exotic places brought the two of us together in the form of Club tours and personal trips that we planned and fulfilled.

One of the letters Maureena wrote to me was instrumental in my fulfilling the dream of a lifetime. She wrote of Tintern Abbey and Wordsworth. A number of years later I was able to ride in an un-tethered hot air balloon.

Many dreams, many good memories all fulfilled with the friendship of a trusted companion. To you Maureena I say thank you and a very Happy Birthday. You are a big part of my life and I always feel a better part of me comes back home from our trips together.

Best Wishes and I'll look forward to being with you again in the near future.
Your friend …Dorothy

Where there is a will …2004

With the promise of riding the Blue Ridge Parkway and Deals Gap, NC the reason to attend Convention was strong. But for a few of our members it was never meant to be.

When disaster strikes, I sometimes wonder what/where the point of no return is, especially this time in the form of three motorcycle accidents. The strength of the will, faith and spirit was put to the ultimate test for three of our ladies that year. They were to attend the 64th Motor Maid Convention in Cherokee, NC. I noticed in different ways how the human spirit continued to guide these Ladies even though all three suffered extreme pain.

I saw the willingness to go on and it wasn't something someone told them how they were going to do, they just did it.

They also knew with faith and hard work and a lot of help they would be back. Doing what they had to do, to live their life and ride again.

To get there they had to have the spirit. Knowing it would take all the strength they had in them, in order to function the same again. What other way was there?

The three Ladies would handle their difficulties differently. One was angry and was going to find ways to resolve another person's poor decision. Monetarily she will have the law to help her with the damage done to her and her bike. Someone else was at fault and now she is the one hurting from the pain inflicted by him. Only fair, the phrase, 'you get -what you give' sounds so appropriate. Another is questioning if there was more damage caused then was first discovered but has

131

decided she will deal with it and will heal. The third put all her strength into another form. She knows hers was a freak accident and also found out she will have to endure many months of hard work and pain but she is willing.

What drives people to go on in such difficult times? I believe for some there is a 'Higher Being' that assists when the mind and body are put to the ultimate test. In the 'Higher Being', faith is in the body and with hard work, the body will heal.

There is also the will of the mind giving strength to continue. Most of all I believe the 'Higher Being' is the soul of the spirit and is there for the asking. We all have it. The combined three are powerful and as a woman, most of us know somehow we'll handle what life puts before us. We've suffered through different degrees of pain during childbirth, perhaps a marriage break down or the death of a child and survived. These Ladies know they will this time too.

They have friends and family who care and that will give them strength during the tough times ahead. In this case, it's not the ride that counts, it's the destination and those who care, hope to be there to see that day. I plan on being there.

Remembering the Fallen

This Saturday morning, I was headed to a meeting of riders with no clue where their ride that day would take me. As advertised in our local paper, a club would be meeting at 11:00am at the local Husky Truck Centre in St. Catharines Ontario. I wanted to ride.

I arrived early to see the group getting ready to leave at the aforementioned time. I was quickly informed we were headed to Queens Park in Toronto to attend a Memorial to honour the Fallen, riders who died an untimely death while riding Motorcycles.

Queens Park is a building that houses the Legislative Assembly of Ontario. Members of the Provincial Parliament from across the Provinces come together to talk about issues, make decisions, pass laws and has often times been the center of rallies and disputes with the Government. The building is bound on all sides with an unobstructed view of Toronto. It has an open area south of the building with extensive tree cover often used for public gatherings and demonstrations.

As we arrived, bikes were still coming in from all directions, with as many already parked in front of Queens Park. Not many police cars were visible. This was a Memorial and a solemn feeling in the air was most apparent. Clubs I recognized included The Southern Cruisers, Abate, M.A.D.D. plus a few Motor Maids.

The memorial itself was in the shape of a tri-fold wooden book. Names of the departed Riders were hand written by their friends and loved ones. I wrote Nancy's name in the book too, having no idea that morning, I would be mourning her loss - again.

133

The service was simple with prayers and the chiming of a bell for each name in the book. During the service, friends stood beside the book to tell all, what their friend meant to them. I wasn't able at this time but I would the next, if I had the chance.

My friend was a Motor Maid and an International Motorcycle Touring Club member. We'd traveled a number of times together overseas and when she met her untimely death, we were both headed to Arizona *(from different directions)* for our Motor Maid Convention in Show Low.

Nancy was a great rider. She was part owner of a bike shoppe in Florida, a former teacher and a friend. She had a curiosity that took us on roads not on our itinerary and she was fun to be with. I have such good memories of our times together and to see her name on a wooden memorial saddened an otherwise fine day. I miss Nancy's humour, her curiosity, her sense of adventure - I miss her.

Motorcycle Riders are committed and loyal. We all are in tune to the possibilities that there for the Grace of God, our names might be written on a piece of wood. There is a special feeling knowing this loyalty and for those who don't understand, there is no point trying to explain it.

Starting the New Year right…01/01/05

New Years Day, bright and beautiful and with nothing planned, it could be a great way to start a year. I can do anything I want. No one expects me. I don't have to answer the phone and if I should want to just turn the world off – I'm free, I can do it!

I dressed warm even though it was bright outside, it was cool. I grabbed my camera and wandered the neighborhood for anything that caught my attention. I eventually stop at a graveyard a road or two away from my home. At this time (9:00am) the lighting is almost perfect.

Looking at the monuments, it's not difficult to be caught up in the sorrow. The architecture and design of the stones was interesting and could be inspiring. Angels gracing the stones showed with faith, there could be hope in the hereafter and short words spoke of a sadness only time would take care of.

Wandering around the grounds I chanced upon a children's burial site situated in the older section of the graveyard showing little attendance to maintenance. In this special section there were tiny stone and wooden crosses with a fenced-off playing area around one. But even sadder was a small marker with one word, 'Child' telling this little one had only lived on this earthly plain a few days. Propped beside it was a stuffed toy.

Pictures can say a thousand words but the few that came to mind at that moment for me, "parents shouldn't have to bury their children." *In my own life I would come to know that life isn't fair – sometimes.*

135

After a number of photos were taken I thought if I could walk in the sun, I could ride in the sun. Who says dates have anything to do with how or when you ride? It's all about the weather. To ride in cooler weather for me is an aphrodisiac. The more I do, the more I want to, even if it's New Years Day in the sunny North.

Living in Canada that drug is withdrawn during the winter months so if you're smart you grab what is available, so…

I hurried home, asked Frank to start the 'Ghost' while I changed into warm riding clothes and electric gloves (an absolute must). I had to get out there before the sun disappeared.

Once dressed and warm, the only hurdle is our *long*, messy, gravel driveway. There are other words to describe the driveway but they're not printable.

Before leaving, I made calls to a few girls to join me and one said 'yes' and I was on my way! I rode along the Niagara Parkway and stopped in the village of Chippawa at Tim Horton's (of course) for a coffee and met my friend. We spoke for a few minutes and then readied ourselves for our quick ride home. At the same time as we were leaving we asked a passerby to take our photo, to document this day. His curiosity of our riding in such cool weather prompted him to ask us a few questions and then he took the photo and we were on our way home in different directions.

My friend said later that as she rode home on the Queen Elizabeth Highway, her hands were so cold it was difficult to shift gears. She doesn't own electric gloves (the *best creation since sliced bread!)*

After the ride, the cobwebs were gone and I felt alive again. It WAS cool and my fingers felt the wind chill factor even with the electric gloves but who could fault us for wanting to get out one more time?

I met two riders on my way home and I'm sure they were thinking the same as I. One more brave soul or another masochist – I would want to think they were the same and would travel in any weather to get that fix.

The next day everything turned white again – and finally the 'Ghost' was put away for a rest.

2006 One year later...

If canceling my attendance at Convention this year (2006) in Kingston would have been an option, I would have, but as Vice President, Publicity chair and Eastern Canada's historian, I felt I couldn't give myself that choice. I never dreamed that so much could have happened in such a short period of time and would necessitate my resignation as Vice President.

Sitting before more than 150 club members after our meeting, my resignation has been announced to the Club and I'm falling back into the dark abyss that has taken over my whole being. Motor Maids are surrounding my seat at the head table with an overwhelming show of support and sympathy. The girls are so well meaning but I can't hold back the emotions and tears that won't stop. I wanted out!

I had such high expectations this last year but the reality for me was that the position of VP had far more duties and required more time then I was prepared for. Eventually, I found I was losing part of me that was important including my health, and most precious – my freedom. The knowledge that I had two more years to fulfill my commitment I felt, I couldn't continue at the same pace. It was supposed to be fun and it wasn't any more.

Shortly after my decision was made to resign I received the second shock of my life. I was informed my son had suddenly passed on due to cardiac arrhythmia. I fell into a deeper loss then I could imagine. At first I felt betrayed! He was supposed to take care of me! How could I go on now? I missed him. It hurt so much.

We shared so many sad memories. He was my rock to lean on when we spoke of the unsolved homicide of his Sister 11 years earlier. No

138

one, not even my loving and supportive husband could understand at the same level, the loss that Randy and I felt over Dawns death. I felt so alone but deep down I knew that I was not.

Months later, time has taken care of a number of things including some of the triggers that start the tears. I can even smile at some of the unique situations Randy's death created. One in particular was arriving at the funeral home to see four of his ex and present wives, all in the same room. I'm fortunate that I had a reasonable relationship with all of them. There were moments that might have caused some concern but the sadness of his absence in all of our lives took precedence.

On our bikes, Motor Maids Joan and Arlene accompanied me to the gravesite. On the way, I heard an almost appropriate song by Willie Nelson, "To All the Girls I've Loved Before." To know my son was to love him, although his life could be quite colourful.

It's only been a couple of months since those terrible days. I'm slowly becoming more aware that there can be a life out there, if I stop and 'smell the roses." In my weaker moments I want to go back and know I can't. I can enjoy my grandchildren, nine all together and I am fortunate. I can see my son and daughter anytime in the smiles of their children, and I know they are with me.

My past position as VP reassured me that I was doing something right in the Club, with the confidence and continued support of many Motor Maids. I will continue as before, as an active club member. I just won't be as visible.

I'm sure there will be some days that won't be easy but in time more will be. After all is said and done, with my family and the friends I have in the Motor Maids – why not?

2006 One Moment in Time

It all led up to this moment. My long time dream was always to be at the head of the Convention parade flying the Canadian Flag and it was finally coming true in Kingston 2006.

Twenty plus years of waiting, wishing and wondering if it would ever happen, finally with the election to Vice Presidency this past year I had the key to my dream and it opened the door.

Now here I was riding the 'Ghost' on this special occasion and proudly flying behind me, our Canadian Flag. My white Wing, a red and white flag, looking soooo good!

140

At first I was nervous, not wanting to have this ride less than perfect, but within seconds the calming throaty sound of the Presidents Harley and the quiet purr of the 'Ghost" calmed all the feelings of anxiety I might have.

The parade could have been described as symmetry in motion as the bleep of the Motorcycle Cop's horn leading us, signaled the road captains to move into place at each and every blocked intersection as we approached.

A sea of blue uniforms, white boots and white -gloved ladies on every brand of motorcycle followed the three flags, the Canadian Maple Leaf, The U.S. Stars and Stripes and our Blue and Gray Motor Maid Flag. The sound of the flags flapping in the breeze and the roar of the bikes, signaled to the world the pride we were all feeling that glorious day in Kingston.

With every smile and wave from the crowd and the riders, we all could say at that moment in time we were all proud. Proud of who we were, what we stood for all those years and the Pride of a Club that has withstood the tests of time to tell all.

"We are the Motor Maids, listen to us roar." "We plan on being around for a long time to come…"

A Final thought 6:20am 10/16/06

Thinking about the possibilities in the coming year, reminds me of a time when I could only sit on 'Ole Yaller' and wonder. What would it be like to ride this 1000cc. bike on my own?

In those days (1980's) the what-ifs drove me crazy and sometimes, still do. 'Ole Yaller' was the last vehicle in the driveway I couldn't ride or drive. Curiosity and the challenge to learn, now has me sitting and watching the changing weather. I'm waiting to pick up my newest bike, a 2005, 1800 Gold Wing and bring her home. After so many miles it's time for an upgrade, so it's in with the new and out with the old time again. I have to say 'Ghost' has been the absolute best, and I only hope this new bike will be as kind.

Where did the time go and how much do I have left? No one knows but I do know I can think and plan and aim for the mountains rather than the hills. It's not my personality to accept less. *Aries can be like that.* When life takes an unexpected detour, I can only go with the flow. Meanwhile, I'll dream and keep looking to the future. Dreams do come true.

So in the coming July I'll be off to the next Convention in Idaho... then if possible, on to Cape Flattery, Washington along the Pacific Coast Highway.

Last but not least... ALASKA – I just want to take a picture of the icebergs before they disappear forever...

Oh the memories...

Pristine Viking Ship, Oslo Norway

Mount St. Helena... smoking

Tornado Alley...Minnesota

Highway ribbon through New Mexico

Grossglockner Pass – Austria

Dolomite switchbacks

Pacific Ocean at dawn

Fjords of Norway

Tintern Abbey and a hot air balloon...

50,000 Motorcycles in tiny Port Dover Ontario

Million buffalo in Yellowstone

Stepping over, during Europe's transition in 1992

Dachau and Auschwitz

Monastery in Ireland

Georgian doors of Dublin

Gondola ride in Venice

Flying the red and white...

Stealth Bomber over Poland

Kindness of a passer-by in Ireland... All never to be forgotten...

143

Dorothy Seabourne

About the Author

Early that July morning the temps were already in the high 80's as the 'Silver Ghost' and I began a search for my independence, my confidence and the reason I was leaving early on this trip. Today I was going to get it back. For the first time in my riding career I was breaking from the pack. Twenty-four years and 1/4 million miles logged as a solo rider, I'm now on another journey. No longer would this trip be on hot tarmac. This one would be a paper trail. The title of my book 'I Did You Can Too', I hope will encourage an aging female population that dreams are there for the making. My career began in my early 40's and now into my late 60's, I have toured throughout the United States and Canada as well as Europe. North American trips

144

were the best but riding in Europe took on a whole new dimension of what I called freedom. The Alps and Dolomites gave me a new appreciation of what I searched for but with that also came the appreciation of what I call normal in my life. My driving force has always been curiosity and after various aspects of my travel I am now able to reconnect. Women of all ages and occupations were my traveling companions and I am privileged to call them friends.

This book consists of memories, photographs and anecdotes telling a tale of one's personal evolution while overcoming adversity and fear. The stories all played out on various bikes rented in Europe and Gold Wings in America.

I belong to the oldest ladies motorcycle club in North America, the Motor Maids Inc., and a member of the International Motorcycle Touring Club based in England for many years.

I've read various stories at meetings, presented slide programs at the camera club and public schools and have had articles published in Club Magazines in America and the U.K. I am proud to say I have been a spokesperson for women riders during my riding career.

Throughout our 34 years together my husband Frank, has been wonderfully supportive. We live on a farm in the Golden Horseshoe area around Niagara Falls Ontario. I've had two children and now have a total of nine grand-children. I am also an upholsterer who enjoys photography. Writing this book was a long time coming and has been a joy to put together.

It is said that it is not the destination but the journey that matters. I also say that the very best part of my travels has always been coming home. I've been lucky to have both. Now how much better can it get?